REDISCOVER THE J[...]
OF NATURE WITH [...]

THE TRACKER
Tom Brown's classic true story—the most powerful and magical high-spiritual adventure since *The Teachings of Don Juan*

THE SEARCH
The continuing story of *The Tracker*, exploring the ancient art of the new survival

THE VISION
Tom Brown's profound, personal journey into an ancient mystical experience, the Vision Quest

THE QUEST
The acclaimed outdoorsman shows how we can save our planet

THE JOURNEY
A message of hope and harmony for our earth and our spirits— Tom Brown's vision for healing our world

GRANDFATHER
The incredible true story of a remarkable Native American and his lifelong search for peace and truth in nature

AWAKENING SPIRITS
For the first time, Tom Brown shares the unique meditation exercises used by students of his personal Tracker Classes

THE WAY OF THE SCOUT
Tom Brown's newest, most empowering work—a collection of stories illustrating the advanced tracking skills taught to him by Grandfather

AND THE BESTSELLING SERIES
OF TOM BROWN'S FIELD GUIDES

Berkley Books by Tom Brown, Jr.

THE TRACKER (as told to William Jon Watkins)
THE SEARCH (with William Owen)
TOM BROWN'S FIELD GUIDE TO WILDERNESS SURVIVAL
(with Brandt Morgan)
TOM BROWN'S FIELD GUIDE TO NATURE OBSERVATION
AND TRACKING (with Brandt Morgan)
TOM BROWN'S FIELD GUIDE TO CITY AND SUBURBAN
SURVIVAL (with Brandt Morgan)
TOM BROWN'S FIELD GUIDE TO LIVING WITH THE
EARTH (with Brandt Morgan)
TOM BROWN'S FIELD GUIDE TO WILD EDIBLE AND
MEDICINAL PLANTS
TOM BROWN'S FIELD GUIDE TO THE FORGOTTEN
WILDERNESS
TOM BROWN'S FIELD GUIDE TO NATURE AND SURVIVAL
FOR CHILDREN (with Judy Brown)
THE VISION
THE JOURNEY
THE QUEST
GRANDFATHER
AWAKENING SPIRITS
THE WAY OF THE SCOUT

About the Author

At the age of eight, Tom Brown, Jr., began to learn tracking
and hunting from Stalking Wolf, a displaced Apache Indian.
Today Brown is an experienced woodsman whose extraor-
dinary skill has saved many lives, including his own. He
manages and teaches one of the largest wilderness and survival schools in the U.S. and has instructed many law
enforcement agencies and rescue teams.

THE QUEST

TOM BROWN, JR.

BERKLEY BOOKS, NEW YORK

THE QUEST

A Berkley Book / published by arrangement with
the author

PRINTING HISTORY
Berkley trade paperback edition / April 1991
Berkley mass market edition / July 1996

The Putnam Berkley World Wide Web site address is
http://www.berkley.com

ISBN: 0-425-15381-9

BERKLEY®
Berkley Books are published by The Berkley Publishing Group,
200 Madison Avenue, New York, New York 10016.
BERKLEY and the "B" design
are trademarks belonging to Berkley Publishing Corporation.

PRINTED IN THE UNITED STATES OF AMERICA

10 9 8 7 6 5 4 3 2 1

IN MEMORY OF ABIGAIL

Dedicated to my son, Tommy,
and to my grandson, Jake,
who keep me fighting harder to save
what is left of the Earth for them

Special thanks to: my wife, Judy, for helping me weed through countless journals to find the quotes necessary for this book. To my son, Paul, and daughter, Kelly, for their strong love and support. To Lisa, our right-hand lady, for editing and typing. And special thanks to Frank Rochelle, Jr., Frank and Karen Sherwood, and Wanda Terhaar, the greatest instructors any school could have. Most of all, a very special thanks to Uncle Howard Crumm, who first led me to wilderness and started me on my path.

CONTENTS

THE QUEST

Preface

This is a continuation of the story of Stalking Wolf, an old Apache shaman and scout whom I call Grandfather. He is not my real grandfather but a spiritual one. For ten years of my life, starting when I was seven years old and continuing until I was eighteen, I spent all my free time with him. Rick, his grandson, and I spent every day after school and weekends with him in the woods. As we got older we spent entire summers together. Grandfather had come to visit the Pine Barrens as a result of a command from his Vision, and there he found Rick and me, in the way that his Vision had foretold. Grandfather had wandered through North and South America for sixty-three years, trying to understand all the old ways and to simplify the philosophy of the earth.

When I met him by the river, Grandfather was then eighty-three and I was seven. The age and cultural differences had little effect on our friendship. Though he could hardly speak English, we understood each other well. For most of the ten years that followed, he taught me to survive

1

in the wilderness lavishly, making all my own tools, shelter, clothing, and gathering food. He taught me how to track and observe the wilderness and to become part of its life force, a process he called "oneness." Most of all, he taught me the spiritual laws of creation. His lessons every day taught the things of the unseen and eternal, to the degree that the spiritual life became more real than the life of the flesh.

After Grandfather went back to his people I began to wander this country for ten years. I lived off the land, tracked animals, observed the wilderness, studied nature, and sought the things of the spirit. Most of the time I stayed to myself, returning home for short periods of time, only to be gone again on another adventure. I practiced diligently all the things Grandfather had taught me, and learned from all the elders and teachers I encountered in my travels. Most of all, I learned from the Earth, as did the Native Americans, for my teacher became Nature itself. I also used my gift and skill for tracking to find lost people, criminals, and in many other types of tracking situations.

I came out of the woods after ten years of wandering and met Judy. Shortly afterward we married. Along with the joy of Judy's two children, we were blessed with our son, Tommy. Then came the book about my life and a flourishing school. My dream had always been to take my family and go back to the wilderness, but I must stay in society and live my Vision. For my Vision is to teach. In that time I have written three books about my life, and seven on the skills that I learned from Grandfather and on my own. This book, *The Quest*, is the first book of a spiritual trilogy.

Introduction

The spirit of wilderness, born into those who seek the quiet places in the temples of creation, unencumbered by the shackles and comforts of society, is the only reality. We escape to the wilderness to find truth, enlightenment, and peace—that separate reality of existence, where everything is pure and natural. Man becomes real, fulfilling his destiny, nourishing his soul, and touching the Creator with every step. But soon man must come back to society to live his Vision and to share the wisdom of the wilderness. It is the coming back that begins man's real quest, the quest of living a life of purity amid all that is artificial and polluted. Living the reality of wilderness in a place that is superficial, sterile, and wrought by the maddening pace of man's ignorance and destruction, that living hell is a place where the truth is distorted and where lives are bought and sold for the good of money, where external accumulations become the temples of the flesh and the spirit is banished to the wasteland of complacency.

This then is the quest, the quest of the living Vision.

This book is a journey, a journey of flesh and spirit, from the world of the purity of wilderness to that which is impure, distorted, and destructive; the world of modern society. It is a book about the teachings of Grandfather and about Vision. It teaches us how to live in society so that our Vision becomes reality and is made manifest in all those lives we touch. It is difficult for anyone who loves wilderness to come back to the world of society, and it is the toughest path a man or woman can walk.

This book deals with the many reasons that one should come out of wilderness, and why. The decision to leave a life of purity and enter a world that is impure and removed from the spiritual rapture is one of the most difficult choices a person must make in his or her life. Once back in society and living the Vision, the road is difficult, and we find that we are walking a knife. On one side of the blade is wilderness, on the other is society, and we become the bridge. To fall from the edge cuts us deeply, and it becomes difficult to climb back up, sometimes impossible.

The question I am most often asked by students is, "How can I take what I learned here in wilderness back home with me into society? How can I continue to live what I have found in the purity of creation?" This book attempts to answer that question through Grandfather's teachings, through the teaching of the Vision, and through my own experience. It then becomes a workbook and guide for all of those who are attempting to live in society with a wilderness mind. As with all my books, *The Quest* is written in the language of the coyote. There is the superficial veneer of meaning, and beneath that obvious lesson lay many others. The reader must look deep into and between the lines to understand, possibly even needing to read things two or three times before all the levels of teaching are known.

This, then, is a guidebook for living in modern society without compromising your Vision or straying from your path. It remains one of the most difficult things we must do on both a physical and a spiritual level. But if we are to realize our Vision and bring it to society, we must live within society. To run away to the wilderness is to run from our Vision, our love, and our responsibility to the spirit-that-moves-in-all-things.

1

The Prophecy

Looking back, I can clearly see that Grandfather's prophecies, unlike anything else, had the greatest influence on my life. At the time they had little more effect than to frighten me and cause me to sit up and take notice. It wasn't until after his prophecies began to come true that their haunting impact began to affect me in a very profound way. More than any other person—prophet, religious leader, or psychic—I have ever met, Grandfather's prophecies, on both a major and a minor scale, came true exactly at the time he prophesied, and exactly as he prophesied. With that record I could not help but feel the impact of these prophecies on my life.

Grandfather could foretell the future with tremendous accuracy. Not only could he precisely tell us what would happen in the next moment, day, week, or year, but with the same accuracy he could predict the possible futures for ten years and more away. It wasn't long before I began to keep detailed records of his predictions, along with other notes

I kept on survival skills, tracking, awareness, and things of the spirit. I received from Grandfather hundreds of personal, minor predictions, and well over half have since come true. Along with the minor personal prophecies were a list of one hundred and three major predictions, of which, to date, over sixty-five have become absolutely true, not only in time and place but also in the exact order in which they were predicted to happen.

Grandfather said that there was not future, only possible futures. The now was like the palm of a hand, with each finger being the possible future, and as always, one of the futures was always the most powerful, the way that the main course of events would surely take us. Thus his predictions were of the possible future, which meant that he always left a choice. He said, "If a man could make the right choices, then he could significantly alter the course of the possible future. No man, then, should feel insignificant, for it only takes one man to alter the consciousness of mankind through the spirit-that-moves-in-all-things. In essence, one thought influences another, then another, until the thought is made manifest throughout all of creation. It is the same thought, the same force, that causes an entire flock of birds to change course, as the flock then has one mind."

Out of all the personal and major prophecies that Grandfather foretold, there are four that stand out above all the rest. It is these four that mark the destruction of man and life on Earth as we know it to exist now. Yet Grandfather said that we could still change things, even after the first two prophecies come true, but that there could be no turning back after the third. Now that we have gone well past the second prophecy of destruction, danger and destruction are very apparent, and our only recourse is to work harder to change what has possibly become the inevitable. The urgency that I feel, now more than ever, is a direct result of the second, impossible prophecy coming true. It is the reason that I teach, sometimes with a certain desperation, and constantly with the sense that we are quickly running out of time.

I should have worked harder and with that same desperation at a much earlier date, but like the rest of mankind, it took a strong message to get me motivated. I should have known that these things he prophesied would someday come true, because his personal, minor predictions were coming true daily. He so accurately foretold of Rick's death on a white horse, that I would someday teach, I would have a son, and that taking him into the Pine Barrens for the first time would forever change my life. He predicted the formation of my school, my books, my family, and even the horrible mistakes I would make as I tried to live within society. Yet with all of this coming true on a daily basis, I simply would not believe or accept that the major prophecy of man's destruction would come true, and its reality hit me hard. It was then that the urgency made itself known.

I remember so vividly the night of the four prophecies, as I have become accustomed to calling that night when Grandfather first made us aware of their possibility. We had been with Grandfather for five years at the time and were accustomed to his prophecies and their accuracy. Our ability to understand the things of the spirit world were as sure as our ability to survive and track. Very little of what society calls the paranormal shocked us anymore, because miracles were part of our everyday existence. Grandfather was a living miracle, and so many of the things that he did on a daily basis, sometimes unconsciously, would be considered miraculous by most. Yet as savvy as we were spiritually, the night of the four prophecies shocked us like nothing we had ever experienced before.

We had been hiking all day without much of a break,

making our way to a place where we were going to camp, atop a small hill that I now call Prophecy Hill. It was a typical midsummer hike; hot, humid, and dusty, with no water available along our entire travel route. As usual, we still took time to stop frequently or take side trips to explore various areas along our route. The adventure and exploration kept us fresh and eager, making the fatigue, heat, and thirst hardly factors. Many times along the way Grandfather would stop and teach us—not physical lessons of survival, tracking, or awareness, but lessons dealing with the awareness of spirit. Very often he would discuss the future, and almost as frequently the past, the distant past.

At one point we stopped along the deer trail we were traveling and followed Grandfather through some heavy brush. The trees and shrubs were far different than those throughout the rest of the Pine Barrens, and I immediately knew this place as an old homestead or town of some sort. Even though the buildings had long since rotted away, the plants and trees still marked the spot where civilization had once stood. Passing through several very thick areas, we finally entered a grove of very tall, old sycamore trees. From their branches and up their trunks ran huge vines, the kind one might imagine he'd find in a jungle. In fact, the whole place looked like a jungle, so out of place from the pine, oak, and blueberry that is typical in the Pine Barrens. As we sat down, a deeper spiritual sense of awareness came over me, and it was then that I noticed the gravestones.

This was the place of a very old and probably long-forgotten cemetery, possibly belonging to the town that had once been here. The stones were old, some lay flat on the ground, others stood upright, though none straight. Plants and bushes had overrun many of the stones, and I could barely make out the markings on the stones. The weathering process had worn away many of the names and dates, making them barely readable. At once we were in awe, humbled and reverent in this place of death; at the same time we were amazed that Grandfather had found it so easily. To my knowledge none of us had been there before, nor had Grandfather ever spoken of this graveyard. Yet for some reason he seemed to be drawn to it, knowing that it was there on some unseen spiritual level, at least unseen to us. I suspect now, as I look back, that he knew that it would become a teaching lesson for us.

He walked over to a gravestone that was partially hidden by foxgrape vines and gently pulled them away. After a long moment he motioned us to come over. We could barely make out the name on the grave or the dates, but at the bottom was carved clearly, "12 years old." Grandfather then spoke. "Who are these people; who is this boy? What did they work for and what were their hopes, dreams, and Visions? Did they just work physically or did they work for the things beyond the flesh, for a grander purpose? Certainly they affected the spirit-that-moves-in-all-things, but did they really work to the best of their ability to make things better for the future of their grandchildren, or did they do nothing other than to perpetuate the myth of society? Were they happy, joyous, and filled with spiritual rapture, or did they just lead lives of labor and mediocrity? And did this young boy live close to the Earth and the Creator, or did he just give up his youth, his sense of adventure, to toil, as did his parents and their parents before them? This boy was exactly your age, and I suspect he had hopes and dreams much like yours. But this is his legacy, lying in a forgotten grave."

"But, Grandfather," I said, "Isn't it enough just to be happy and live your life fully?"

After a long moment of silence Grandfather answered, "It is not enough that man be just happy in the flesh, but he must also be happy and joyous in spirit. For without spiritual happiness, and rapture, life is shallow. Without seeking the things of the spirit, life is half lived and empty. And by spiritual life I do not mean just setting aside one hour of one day of one week for worship but to seek the things of the spirit every moment of every day. I ask you, then, what did these people do to seek spiritual enlightenment and rapture? Did they just give in to a life that was little more than work? They were given a choice every day of their lives, as you will be given a choice, to seek the rapture of the spirit or to resign yourselves to a life of meaningless work. The end result is always the same: forgotten graves and forgotten dreams of forgotten people. It is not important that anyone notice or remember but that you work to touch God, and affect, in a positive way, the consciousness of the spirit-that-moves-in-all-things, thus bringing the consciousness of man closer to the Creator.''

We left the graveyard without a word and headed up to the campsite on the hill. By the time we reached the camp it had cooled off, and the sun had long since set. As we built shelters, a fire, and gathered food, time seemed to fly by unnoticed, as my mind was thoroughly engrossed in thoughts of the lessons in the graveyard. I wondered how much I might be like that nameless dead boy in that forgotten grave. Was I just seeking the flesh and not working hard enough in the things of the spirit? It was then that I realized the deeper lessons of what Grandfather was trying to teach me. I realized then that I should live life as if I were to die tomorrow, for that is what happened to that young boy. No one can be assured of another day, but we must live each day fully, in flesh and most of all in spirit. It isn't important that anyone remember who we were but that we made a positive change in the consciousness of the spirit-that-moves-in-all-things, the life force of the Earth, and in doing so find spiritual rapture and touch the Creator.

I sat by the fire after the work was done, relaxing, still deep in thought about the boy in the graveyard. Grandfather sat at the far end of the fire, his eyes closed, but I suspected that he was not sleeping. In the firelight his features appeared more that of a spirit than of flesh. Quietly he leaned forward and answered the many questions I had on my mind. At times his ability to know what was on my mind was unnerving, at times making me angry to think that he could know my thoughts.

"Did you ever watch a flock of sandpipers on the beach, how they ebb and flow with the tides, becoming at times not a gathering of individual animals but one organism, moving as a unit together along the surf? When they burst into flight, their cohesiveness is even more startling and wondrous. At once they all will be flying in a certain direction, and then in an instant the entire flock will turn simultaneously and take a new direction.

"Studied closely, there is no one bird that makes the decision to turn, but it seems to be a spirit, a collective consciousness that runs through the flock instantly. When viewed from afar, the flock appears to be one animal, one organism, one consciousness, governed by the collective force and spirit of all the individuals. It is this same consciousness that runs through man, nature, and the Earth, that which we call the spirit-that-moves-in-all-things, or the life force.

"I suspect," he continued, "that it is but one bird that creates the thought that turns the flock, and the one thought becomes immediately manifested in all the others. The individual then transcends self and becomes one with the whole. Thus, at once, the bird moves within the flock and the flock moves within the bird. So then do not ask what you can do to affect the life force in a positive way, for the same spirit that moves within the birds also moves within you. One person, one idea, one thought can turn the flock of society away from the destructive path of modern times. It is not a question as to whether we make a difference, for we all make a difference, each of us in our own way. It is the difference we make that is important.''

''So if we live a life that is close to the spirit, seek the spiritual rapture of oneness, that will affect the outcome of life,'' I said. My statement was more a question than a declaration.

''It is not enough,'' Grandfather said, ''just to seek the things of the spirit on a personal level. To do so is selfish, and those who just seek the spiritual realms for themselves are not working to change the spirit that moves through the consciousness of man. Instead they are running away, hiding from their responsibility, and using their wisdom for their own glorification. Spiritual man must then work for a principal, a cause, a quest, far greater then the glorification of self, in order to affect the spirit that can change the course of man's destruction.''

I sat for a long time in the quietude of the night, trying desperately to understand what Grandfather had told me. In essence it was not enough to work for spiritual enlightenment for self but to work for the spiritual enlightenment of all of mankind. To work only for self, to cloister oneself in the seeking of spiritual rapture, is to run from this responsibility. What Grandfather was saying is that a spiritual person must take the wisdom and philosophy of the Earth and bring it back into modern society.

Grandfather spoke again, saying, ''Trying to live a spiritual life in modern society is the most difficult path one can walk. It is a path of pain, of isolation, and of shaken faith, but that is the only way that our Vision can become reality. Thus the true Quest in life is to live the philosophy of the Earth within the confines of man. There is no church or temple we need to seek peace, for ours are the temples of the wilderness. There are no spiritual leaders, for our hearts and the Creator are our only leaders. Our numbers are scattered; few speak our language or understand the things that we live. Thus we walk this path alone, for each Vision, each Quest, is unique unto the individual. But we must walk within society or our Vision dies, for a man not living his Vision is living death."

For a long time there was no other conversation. I retired into my own thoughts and doubts. I did not want to live within society, for the wilderness was my home, my love, my life, and my spiritual rapture. I could not see why a man could not live his Vision in the purity of wilderness, away from the distractions of society. I could feel no urgency, or any reason why I should take what I have learned back to society.

Grandfather's voice shattered my thoughts, saying, "The Earth is dying. The destruction of man is close, so very close, and we must all work to change that path of destruction. We must pay for the sins of our grandfathers and grandmothers, for we have long been a society that kills its grandchildren to feed its children. There can be no rest, and we cannot run away; far too many in the past have run away. It is very easy to live a spiritual life away from man, but the truth of Vision, in spiritual life, can only be tested and become a reality when lived near society."

"How do I know that we are so close to that destruction?" I asked. "I had a Vision," Grandfather said. "It was a Vision of the destruction of man. But man was given four warnings to that destruction, two of which gave man a chance to change his ways and two of which would give the children of the Earth time to escape the Creator's wrath."

"How will I know these warnings, these signs?" I asked.

Grandfather continued, "They will be obvious to you and those who have learned to listen to the spirit of the Earth, but to those who live within the flesh and know only flesh, there is no knowing or understanding. When these signs, these warnings and prophecies, are made manifest, then you will understand the urgency of what I speak. Then you will understand why people must not just work for their own spiritual rapture but to bring that rapture to the consciousness of modern man."

Grandfather had been wandering for several years and was well into his forties when the Vision of the four signs were given to him. He had just finished his third Vision Quest at the Eternal Cave when the Vision made itself known. He had been seated at the mouth of the cave, awaiting the rising sun, when the spirit of the warrior appeared to him. He felt as if he were in a state somewhere between dream and reality, sleep and wakefulness, until the spirit finally spoke and he knew that it was not his imagination. The spirit called Grandfather's name and beckoned him to follow. As Grandfather stood, he was suddenly transported to another world. Again he thought that he was dreaming, but his flesh could feel the reality of this place; his senses knew that this was a state of abject reality but in another time and place.

The spirit warrior spoke to Grandfather, saying, "These are the things yet to come that will mark the destruction of man. These things you may never see, but you must work to stop them and pass these warnings on to your grandchildren. They are the possible futures of what will come if man does not come back to the Earth and begin to obey the laws of Creation and the Creator. There are four signs, four warnings, that only the children of the Earth will understand. Each warning marks the beginning of a possible future, and as each warning becomes reality, so, too, does the future it marks.'' With that the spirit warrior was gone and Grandfather was left alone in this strange new world.

The world he was in was like nothing he had ever known. It was a dry place, with little vegetation. In the distance he saw a village, yet it was made out of tents and cloth rather than from the materials of the Earth. As he drew closer to the village the stench of death overwhelmed him and he grew sick. He could hear children crying, the moaning of elders, and the sounds of sickness and despair. Piles of bodies lay in open pits awaiting burial, their contorted faces and frail bodies foretelling of death from starvation. The bodies appeared more like skeletons than flesh, and children, adults, and elders all looked the same, their once dark brown complexions now ash gray.

As Grandfather entered the village, the horror of living starvation struck him deeper. Children could barely walk, elders lay dying, and everywhere were the cries of pain and fear. The stench of death and the sense of hopelessness overwhelmed Grandfather, threatening to drive him from the village. It was then that an elder appeared to Grandfather, at first speaking in a language that he could not understand. Grandfather realized as the elder spoke that he was the spirit of a man, a man no longer of flesh but a man that had once walked a spiritual path, possibly a shaman of this tribe. It was then that he understood what the old one was trying to tell him.

The elder spoke softly, saying, ''Welcome to what will be called the land of starvation. The world will one day look upon all of this with horror and will blame the famine on the weather and the Earth. This will be the first warning to the world that man cannot live beyond the laws of Creation, nor can he fight Nature. If the world sees that it is to blame for this famine, this senseless starvation, then a great lesson will be learned. But I am afraid that the world will not blame itself but that the blame will be placed on Nature. The world will not see that it created this place of death by forcing these people to have larger families. When the natural laws of the land were broken, the people starved, as Nature starves the deer in winter when their numbers are too many for the land to bear.''

The old one continued. ''These people should have been left alone. They once understood how to live with the Earth, and their wealth was measured in happiness, love, and peace. But all of that was taken from them when the world saw theirs as a primitive society. It was then that the world showed them how to farm and live in a less primitive way. It was the world that forced them to live outside the laws of creation and as a result is now forcing them to die.'' The old man slowly began to walk away, back to the death and despair. He turned one last time to Grandfather and said, ''This will be the first sign. There will come starvation before and after this starvation, but none will capture the attention of the world with such impact as does this one. The children of the Earth will know the lessons that are held in all of this pain and death, but the world will only see it as drought and famine, blaming Nature instead of itself.'' With that the old one disappeared, and Grandfather found himself back at the mouth of the Eternal Cave.

Grandfather lay back on the ground, thinking about what he had witnessed. He knew that it had been a Vision of the possible future and that the spirit of the warrior had brought him to it to teach him what could happen. Grandfather knew that people all over the Earth were now starving, but why was this starvation so critical, so much more important than all the rest, even more important than the starvation that was taking place now? It was then that Grandfather recalled that the tribal elder had said that the entire world would take notice but that the world would not learn the lessons of what the death and famine were trying to teach. The children would die in vain.

Grandfather looked out across the barren land that surrounded the Eternal Cave to try to reestablish the reality of his now. He said that it was still hard to discern between waking reality and the world of Vision, but he felt that he was back into his time and place. He told me that the Eternal Cave was always a place to find Visions of the possible and probable futures, and it was not uncommon for the searcher to have Vision at the mouth of the cave and not just inside. In a state of physical and emotional exhaustion, Grandfather fell into a deep sleep, but it was in this sleep that the warrior spirit appeared to him again and brought the remainder of the first sign to completion.

In his dream the spirit spoke to Grandfather, saying, "It is during the years of the famine, the first sign, that man will be plagued by a disease, a disease that will sweep the land and terrorize the masses. The doctors (white coats) will have no answers for the people and a great cry will arise across the land. The disease will be born of monkeys, drugs, and sex. It will destroy man from inside, making common sickness a killing disease. Mankind will bring this disease upon himself as a result of his life, his worship of sex and drugs, and a life away from Nature. This, too, is a part of the first warning, but again man will not heed this warning and he will continue to worship the false gods of sex and the unconscious spirit of drugs."

The spirit continued, saying, "The drugs will produce wars in the cities of man, and the nations will arise against those wars, arise against that killing disease. But the nations will fight in the wrong way, lashing out at the effect rather than the cause. It will never win these wars until the nation, until society, changes its values and stops chasing the gods of sex and drugs. It is then, in the years of the first sign, that man can change the course of the probable future. It is then that he may understand the greater lessons of the famine and the disease. It is then that there can still be hope. But once the second sign of destruction appears, the Earth can no longer be healed on a physical level. Only a spiritual healing can then change the course of the probable futures of mankind.'' With that the warrior spirit let Grandfather fall into a deep and dreamless sleep, allowing him to rest fully before any more Vision was wrought upon him.

Grandfather awoke at the entrance of the cave once again, the memory of the warrior spirit still vivid in his mind, the spirit's words becoming part of his soul. When Grandfather looked out across the landscape, all had changed. The landscape appeared drier, there was no vegetation to be seen, and animals lay dying. A great stench of death arose from the land, and the dust was thick and choking, the intense heat oppressive. Looking skyward, the sun seemed to be larger and more intense; no birds or clouds could be seen; and the air seemed thicker still. It was then that the sky seemed to surge and huge holes began to appear. The holes tore with a resounding, thunderous sound, and the very Earth, rocks, and soil shook.

The skin of the sky seemed to be torn open like a series of gaping wounds, and through these wounds seeped a liquid that seemed like the oozing of an infection, a great sea of floating garbage, oil, and dead fish. It was through one of these wounds that Grandfather saw the floating bodies of dolphins, accompanied by tremendous upheavals of the Earth and of violent storms. As he held fast to the trembling Earth his eyes fell from the sky, and all about him, all at once, was disaster. Piles of garbage reached to the skies, forests lay cut and dying, coastlines flooded, and storms grew more violent and thunderous. With each passing moment the Earth shook with greater intensity, threatening to tear apart and swallow Grandfather.

Suddenly the Earth stopped shaking and the sky cleared. Out of the dusty air walked the warrior spirit, who stopped a short distance from Grandfather. As Grandfather looked into the face of the spirit he could see that there were great tears flowing from his eyes, and each tear fell to the Earth with a searing sound. The spirit looked at Grandfather for a long moment, then finally spoke, saying, "Holes in the sky." Grandfather thought for a moment, then, in a questioning, disbelieving manner, said, "Holes in the sky?" And the spirit answered, saying, "They will become the second sign of the destruction of man. The holes in the sky and all that you have seen could become man's reality. It is here, at the beginning of this second sign, that man can no longer heal the Earth with physical action. It is here that man must heed the warning and work harder to change the future at hand. But man must not only work physically, he must also work spiritually, through prayer, for only through prayer can man now hope to heal the Earth and himself."

There was a long pause as Grandfather thought about the impossibility of holes in the sky. Surely Grandfather knew that there could be a spiritual hole, but a hole that the societies of the Earth could notice would hardly seem likely. The spirit drew closer and spoke again, almost in a whisper. "These holes are a direct result of man's life, his travel, and of the sins of his grandfathers and grandmothers. These holes, the second sign, will mark the killing of his grandchildren and will become a legacy to man's life away from nature. It is the time of these holes that will mark a great transition in mankind's thinking. They will then be faced with a choice, a choice to continue following the path of destruction or a choice to move back to the philosophy of the Earth and a simpler existence. It is here that the decision must be made, or all will be lost.'' Without another word the spirit turned and walked back into the dust.

Grandfather spent the next four days at the cave entrance, though for those four days nothing spoke to him, not even the Earth. He said that it was a time of great sorrow, of aloneness, and a time to digest all that had taken place. He knew that these things would not appear in his lifetime, but they had to be passed down to the people of the future, with the same urgency and power with which they had been delivered to him. But he did not know how he would explain these unlikely events to anyone. Surely the elders and shamans of the tribes would understand, but not society, and certainly not anyone who was removed from the Earth and spirit. He sat for the full four days, unmoving, as if made of stone, and his heart felt heavy with the burden he now carried.

It was at the end of the fourth day that the third Vision came to him. As he gazed out onto the landscape toward the setting sun, the sky suddenly turned back to a liquid and then turned blood red. As far as his eyes could see, the sky was solid red, with no variation in shadow, texture, or light. The whole of creation seemed to have grown still, as if awaiting some unseen command. Time, place, and destiny seemed to be in limbo, stilled by the bleeding sky. He gazed for a long time at the sky, in a state of awe and terror, for the red color of the sky was like nothing he had ever seen in any sunset or sunrise. The color was that of man, not of Nature, and it had a vile stench and texture. It seemed to burn the Earth wherever it touched. As sunset drifted to night, the stars shone bright red, the color never leaving the sky, and everywhere was heard the cries of fear and pain.

Again the warrior spirit appeared to Grandfather, but this time as a voice from the sky. Like thunder, the voice shook the landscape, saying, "This, then, is the third sign, the night of the bleeding stars. It will become known throughout the world, for the sky in all lands will be red with the blood of the sky, day and night. It is then, with this sign of the third probable future, that there is no longer hope. Life on the Earth as man has lived it will come to an end, and there can be no turning back, physically or spiritually. It is then, if things are not changed during the second sign, that man will surely know the destruction of the Earth is at hand. It is then that the children of the Earth must run to the wild places and hide. For when the sky bleeds fire, there will be no safety in the world of man."

Grandfather sat in shocked horror as the voice continued. "From this time, when the stars bleed, to the fourth and final sign will be four seasons of peace. It is in these four seasons that the children of the Earth must live deep in the wild places and find a new home, close to the Earth and the Creator. It is only the children of the Earth that will survive, and they must live the philosophy of the Earth, never returning to the thinking of man. And survival will not be enough, for the children of the Earth must also live close to the spirit. So tell them not to hesitate if and when this third sign becomes manifest in the stars, for there are but four seasons to escape." Grandfather said that the voice and red sky lingered for a week and then were gone as quickly as they were manifest.

Grandfather did not remember how many days he'd spent at the mouth of the cave, nor did it make a difference, for he had received the Vision he had come for. It was in his final night at the Eternal Cave that the fourth Vision came to Grandfather, this time carried by the voice of a young child. The child spoke, saying, "The fourth and final sign will appear through the next ten winters following the night that the stars will bleed. During this time the Earth will heal itself and man will die. For those ten years the children of the Earth must remain hidden in the wild places, make no permanent camps, and wander to avoid contact with the last remaining forces of man. They must remain hidden, like the ancient scouts and fight the urge to go back to the destruction of man. Curiosity could kill many.''

There was a long silence, until Grandfather spoke to the child spirit, asking, ''And what will happen to the worlds of man?'' There was another period of silence until finally the child spoke again. ''There will be a great famine throughout the world, like man cannot imagine. Waters will run vile, the poisons of man's sins running strong in the waters of the soils, lakes, and rivers. Crops will fail, the animals of man will die, and disease will kill the masses. The grandchildren will feed upon the remains of the dead, and all about will be the cries of pain and anguish. Roving bands of men will hunt and kill other men for food, and water will always be scarce, getting scarcer with each passing year. The land, the water, the sky will all be poisoned, and man will live in the wrath of the Creator. Man will hide at first in the cities, but there he will die. A few will run to the wilderness, but the wilderness will destroy them, for they had long ago been given a choice. Man will be destroyed, his cities in ruin, and it is then that the grandchildren will pay for the sins of their grandfathers and grandmothers.''

''Is there then no hope?'' Grandfather asked.

The child spoke again. ''There is only hope during the time of the first and second signs. Upon the third sign, the night of the bleeding, there is no longer hope, for only the children of the Earth will survive. Man will be given these warnings; if unheeded, there can be no hope, for only the children of the Earth will purge themselves of the cancers of mankind, of mankind's destructive thinking. It will be the children of the Earth who will bring a new hope to the new society, living closer to the Earth and spirit.''

Then all was silent, the landscape cleared and returned to normal, and Grandfather stepped from the Vision. Shaken, he said that he had wandered for the next season, trying to understand all that had been given to him, trying to understand why he had been chosen.

Grandfather had related the story to me in great detail during that night of the four prophecies. I don't think that any event had been left out, and his emotions and thoughts were such that he actually relived it for us. Thus the power of his Vision became part of our spirit, our driving force, and a big part of our fears. I sat for a long time up on the hill. The fire had gone out, and all had retired to sleep for the night. Creation seemed to be at a standstill, awaiting this darkest part of the night to pass by. I felt alone and vulnerable, as if all of creation were scrutinizing my every thought. I had no idea what to do with what Grandfather had given me through his Vision . How could I ever make a difference or make anyone understand the Vision of another?

Grandfather had had this Vision sometime in the 1920s, and now it was 1962, and still there were no great famines, and certainly no holes in the sky. I wondered how we could ever tell if there was a hole in the sky or not, for certainly the air was transparent and there could be no way to see a hole in air. I laughed to myself at a fleeting image of Chicken Little running around the barnyard shouting, ''The sky is falling!'' Certainly I would look just as insane, going around shouting that there were holes in the sky. The whole thing seemed so farfetched, so impossible. Granted, Grandfather had been right in all of his other prophecies, but these were bizarre, even for him. Somewhere in that thought I drifted off into what I thought was a sound sleep.

I awoke to the deepest blackness of the night, startled, and feeling that someone, something, was watching me. I glanced around the parts of the landscape that I could vaguely see, but there was nothing, not a sound, only the feeling of being watched. It was then that I looked up into the sky and saw the bloodred stars shining down through a huge gaping hole, a hole that seemed to be torn from the permeable fabric of the sky. I was pinned to the ground, unable to move, my fear rising in my throat, making it difficult for me to breathe. I knew now that surely this must be the end, the final sign taking hold. Grandfather's prophecy had come true. I grew violently sick to my stomach but could not retch. My body became numb, cold, and beaded with sweat. I tried to call for Grandfather or Rick, but my scream was silent.

A voice broke the silence, a voice much like Grandfather's but different. It sounded as if Grandfather had grown twenty years older and more hoarse. It spoke to me, saying, "How can you not believe the holes in the sky, the stars that bleed, or the famine? You have borne witness to the impossible before, and you see the impossible happen each day, all around you, yet you say that you cannot believe. As you have lived, you have known that faith is the most powerful force on Earth and in the heavens, faith knows no fact or reason, transcends the laws of science—faith is the most powerful. Because you cannot understand how these things can happen, or how to bear witness of these things, your faith is shaken and you cannot fully accept them. This same young warrior, who has lived in the temples of the wilderness and touched God, who has seen and lived the power of Vision and spirit, now cannot comprehend the prophecies set before you? Why, then, can you not now transcend flesh and mind and accept these things?"

I awoke terrorized, frightened more than I had ever remembered being in my life. I ran blindly from camp, screaming Grandfather's name, trying desperately to leave what I had just dreamed or witnessed, I did not know which. I fell, crashing through the thick brush, and ended up on my back at the bottom of the hill. It was then that I noticed that the stars in the sky were clear and that the landscape had returned to normal. I could see the fissure of dawn appearing on the distant horizon, and I felt whole again. The fear had vanished but I did not know why. What I did notice was a change in my thinking, a deep but subtle change. I had somehow accepted the four prophecies as a possible future reality, and I didn't know how, but somehow I was going to keep them from becoming reality. Relaxed now, I drifted off to sleep, exactly where I had fallen.

The sleep experienced after being physically and spiritually exhausted can be deep and forgetful. I awoke well into the morning, still shaken from the experience of the past night, still in the same place I had fallen. There was a certain clarity to my thinking, and I felt refreshed. I could, however, feel the burden of the four prophecies, but the fear was no longer terror, just a healthy fear that had become a driving force. I wandered back up to the camp, still shaken and sporting a healthy assortment of new scars from my panicked run. Grandfather sat in camp, patiently waiting for me, and I could feel that he knew what had happened to me during the night. Again my thoughts were transparent, and I felt a little humbled because of my disbelief.

Before I spoke, Grandfather hushed me to silence, saying, "You wonder why I have passed down these Visions to you, and what you should do with that knowledge? As I have told you, man must not only work for his own spiritual enlightenment but also for the spiritual enlightenment of all mankind. For to run and hide, to think only of oneself and not to have love and compassion for all of man, is to deny part of self. Man is part of the spirit-that-moves-in-all-things, and when one part of that spirit is sick, then all are sick; and when one part of that spirit dies, then part of self dies. These Visions, these four prophecies, are the things you should work to resolve, things that lie beyond the self. Thus, by working to keep these prophecies and Visions from becoming reality, and to make the world whole again, we become dedicated to something greater than self, and your spiritual life becomes visible and full. You do not run away from your responsibility.''

Grandfather then ended the conversation and wandered out of camp, leaving me to my thoughts. Until this point I had never realized how adamant he was about bringing the philosophy of the Earth out into civilization. Yet Grandfather never ventured very far out of the wilderness, nor did he go out of his way to teach his philosophy, except to a select few individuals. I wondered why he then told me that someday I had to take what I knew out into the world of man when he didn't even follow what he preached. His voice broke the silence of my thoughts, saying, ''The choice to go back to the world of man is not yours or mine; it is the world of spirit that sends us, each to his capacity, each in his own way. I am living my Vision and teaching the way that Vision dictates, and someday you must do the same.''

''But how will I know what to teach, where to go, and who to reach with the teaching?'' I asked.

''The way and the means will be made manifest through Vision and from the direction of the world of the spirit,'' Grandfather said, ''so make no concern about these things, for to a person living beyond his own spiritual selfishness the way will become clear. Thus if a person is attuned to the world of the spirit, the world of Vision, and working for things beyond his- or herself, then the path and time to act becomes clear. Until then, allow the spirit of the Earth and the Creator to teach, and the Vision Quest to guide, and all else will become reality.''

I then told Grandfather that it didn't seem fair that a man could not live his life in wilderness if that was his choice. Grandfather responded emphatically, saying, "In these desperate times, when the Earth is dying, there can be no rest, no running away, for each of us in our own way must work to change the probable future of mankind. For if modern man destroys himself, then we are personally responsible, and we are destroyed also. Each then is accountable for the future.''

We packed, broke camp, and headed back to the Medicine Cabin, following the same route we had originally taken. Grandfather left a few hours later, leaving Rick and me to wander alone without thought. I eventually wandered away from Rick, taking side trips of exploration but never fully living in the flesh. My mind still reeled and floundered over the events of the past night. I wandered almost unconsciously, when I again stumbled upon the grave of the young boy whom Grandfather had pointed out the day before. It was a shock to find myself there, for I had entered the graveyard from a different direction and had no idea exactly where I was. I had the feeling that I had been directed here by some unseen spiritual force, though it was nothing conscious. At the same time I had the desire to spend the night, as morbid as it might sound, but my mind would not accept what my heart was telling me. I soon returned to the path and headed back to the cabin.

I had understood the things Grandfather had taught me that night so long ago, but I would not accept the fact that someday I had to bring the wilderness philosophy back to society. I could understand that man should not seek just the spiritual enlightenment of self, for to do so would be running away from oneself, from the greater self that includes all of man.

For many years I did not feel the urgency of what Grandfather taught, nor could I love my fellowman enough to give up my wilderness and return to society. There was so much that I had yet to learn, and it would be years before I would fully understand the four prophecies. What I essentially did, those many years ago, was to put out of my mind all that had happened on Prophecy Hill and concentrate my efforts on spending as much time as possible in the wilderness.

Still they haunted me, still they taught me, and I could never be free of them, no matter how much I denied them.

2

The Grave

Almost a year after the teaching on Prophecy Hill I found myself drawn back into that area of the Pine Barrens. I had not been there in several months, and that area seemed to be calling me in some strange subliminal way. No matter what I was doing, where I went, or what area I was exploring, I could not get the hill out of my mind. It was like part of me had to go back, for something was missing from the teachings; something else had to be conveyed to me. There was a feeling that there was something left undone, something I desperately needed to know. I had put this feeling off for more than a month, until finally I could take it no more and headed down the long path to Prophecy Hill. I had asked Grandfather to go, but he said that it was my personal calling, not his, and I had to go alone.

The original path we had taken to the hill had overgrown, and the going was difficult. I decided to take another route, doing what the deer and other animals were doing at that time of year, taking a more frequently used trail system. I had never been on that trail system before, but I knew that it would eventually lead me to the cedar swamps just west of our old path, then I could cut across the swamp and get to the hill that way. It was an unspoken law that we never use the trails of man but instead use the trails of animals. We could also never use the same trail twice, always going and coming along different routes. This way we would not wear paths into the land that would someday look like scars. This mode of travel also would take us through the deeper, relatively unexplored parts of the Pine Barrens and close to the heart of creation. The problem with this type of travel was that it is typically very slow and very easy to get lost, though being lost is a state of mind.

It wasn't long before I did become lost. Not that I did not know what direction I was headed, nor that I wouldn't eventually get to my destination, but that I was totally unfamiliar with this part of the Pine Barrens and wasn't sure exactly how far along my route I had traveled. I was beginning to worry that I wouldn't make it to the hill until well after dark, and I feared that the trail had passed the swamp too far to the west, thus bypassing the swamp altogether. Normally I would seek out this feeling of being lost, for being lost puts one closer to the Earth, closer to adventure. In our world, being lost is nothing to fear but something to savor, for when lost, we still have all we need to survive lavishly. How can one ever truly be lost at home? Anyway, Grandfather had a saying: "You are lost only when you have a place to go and a time to be there," and I might add, no survival skills to keep you safe. The draw I felt for the hill was so compelling, so demanding, that I was in a way lost, because I just had to be there.

I began to grow anxious, because it was getting so late and it seemed that I had yet so far to go. I knew that even if I passed several miles west of the swamp, I could have smelled the distant water, but the winds were blowing away from me toward the east. I also could be so far west that I would not notice or hear the birds and wildlife that would foretell the oncoming water. I would have stopped there for the night, but some demanding inner force wanted me on the hill that night. It was then that I took a guess, left the trail, and pushed east, through the heavy brush. I had figured that I must have either passed the swamp or been near enough to get back to the original trail. By pushing directly east, I would eventually intersect with that trail or the swamp. What I didn't figure on was the thickness of the brush and the slow pace it would dictate.

For what seemed forever, I pushed through thick brush and briars to a point of exhaustion. I was still driven by the inner desire to get to Prophecy Hill, which made my pace faster than normal, faster than the landscape allowed. It was easy to keep the general direction, but my route curved back and forth like a snake as I negotiated the easiest routes around the thicker patches of brush. So many times I wanted to stop and explore something along the way, for so much of the landscape was new and exciting, but my quest for the hill overrode any exploration, side trips, or even time to rest. It wasn't long before I was overtaken by night, and soon after sunset a thick sheet of clouds moved in, making it nearly impossible to tell direction. Even the wind shifted frequently, as if it were purposely trying to confuse my sense of direction. In the abyss of darkness my travel was slowed to a crawl or less. So many times I got hung in brush, only to try and struggle to rip free. Even with fox walking and sensing the landscape with my body, the going was nearly impossible. There were just no holes in the brush to get through. I was so angry with myself at this point, for I was going against all that I had been trained to do, including my beliefs. I was traveling too fast, dam-

aging the landscape and my body, like some wounded animal floundering in the woods. I cursed myself for moving
like someone who had never been in the wilderness before.
The anger, instead of making me slow down and travel
quietly, only made me push harder and faster, like I was
punishing myself through pain inflicted by the brush. The
obsession with the hill grew even stronger, as my anger
and stumbling became more intense.

I had now pushed myself to near exhaustion. It was late,
and the brush had taken its toll on my body, mind, and
energy. I pushed on in a daze, only guessing the direction,
fumbling, tripping, and falling more frequently than ever. I
was even too tired and exhausted to get angry at myself,
for what I felt now was embarrassment. How was I going
to tell Grandfather that I had not made it to the hill that
night? How was I ever going to explain the scars on my
body and the new path of destruction I had crashed through
the landscape? I felt so sick, tired, disoriented, and mentally
exhausted. The trip had nearly beaten me. At this point I
was so exhausted mentally and physically that I began to
hallucinate. I imagined pathways up ahead, only to crash
into thicker brush. I heard voices, footfalls, and the distant
drone of machinery. At one point I thought I saw a lantern
in the distance, but when I stopped to carefully listen and
look, all of the images were gone. I was covered with
sweat, my body was scarred, and I was trembling with exhaustion. It was then that I fell to the ground hard, tripping
over some overlooked log, and lay for a long time, gasping,
trembling, and physically spent. The force that drew me to
the hill vanished, and I fell into a deep sleep, unable to go
on.

I awoke abruptly to the sound of a boy's voice—Rick's,
I thought. The morning dew had almost dried, and I figured
that I must have slept for several hours, though I did not

fully remember the sleep. The voice called again, but it was not Rick's voice, as I had originally thought. I had no idea who it was or where it came from. Then I also realized I did not know exactly where I was. I painfully stood up, my muscles sore and stiff from last night's travel; some of the deeper scratches stung. I followed a small, worn path that lay in front of me, trying to find the origin of the boy's voice, more out of curiosity than necessity. I wanted to get back on my route of travel as quickly as possible, but the side trip would squelch my curiosity and hopefully give me an indication of where I was exactly. As far as I could remember, there were no houses and no civilization close to this part of the Pine Barrens.

I walked quietly along the small path, obvious to me now that it hadn't been made by animals but by man. I did not want to run into anyone in the woods, for that would only rob me of the delightful feeling of aloneness and seclusion. I did, however, want to see who would be way out here, this far from any house. As I heard the voice again, the thought came over me that I had traveled too far south and ended up at the edge of some town, but that would have been impossible, given the time and place of my route. The thought of another boy in the woods was intriguing. Possibly he would be interested in the woods, and I could even introduce him to Grandfather. Rick and I would have another friend, I thought. My mind ran unchecked as I deftly moved along the trail, getting closer to the origin of the voice.

The little path opened into a larger trail that showed more frequency of travel, travel by man. I instinctively slowed to a crawl and hugged the trail close to the thicker brush, as did the ancient Apache scouts when avoiding detection. The trail eventually ended at the edge of a clearing that was bordered on one end by a large pond. At the far end of the clearing I could barely make out a house and several out-buildings. All were neat and almost entirely hidden by thickets of brush, though it was evident that they were well cared for and relatively new. I noticed also that they were made out of cedar, something that was rarely used anymore in modern houses. It was then that I heard the boy's voice again, coming from the direction of the pond. I jumped from the trail and cut through the heavy brush at the edge of the field, careful to make no sound or quick movement. Eventually I worked my way to the light brush at the edge of the pond, crawling the last several feet to the edge. I wanted to get a look at the young boy without being de-tected.

It wasn't that I was afraid of encountering anyone new in the woods, but I was basically a loner and did not like running into anyone unexpectedly or getting into a situation where I wasn't aware of what was going on. Anytime noise or people were heard in the wilderness, they were first checked out and scrutinized from a distance, then usually avoided. I just did not like to socialize or go out of my way to talk to people. Rarely did they speak my language or understand the wilderness, so conversation and encoun-ters, if any, were rare indeed. I also enjoyed the act of stalking and observing anything in the wilderness, and even man was fair game. It was much like the stealth and aware-ness of the ancient Apache scouts checking on potential danger. It was important to know exactly where everything was in the woods, and, not wanting to break tradition or to allow my curiosity to get the better of me, I stalked to the pond.

As I got to the thick, lower brush at the edge of the pond, I could hear the boy's voice again, coming from the far bank. With a few short and quiet maneuvers I had the boy in clear view. He was about my age, very tanned from the sun, and quite muscular. He lay on his belly, trying to approach a large bullfrog at the edge of the pond. I lay there watching him for the better part of an hour as he attempted and failed repeatedly to stalk the frog. With practice and patience, none like I had ever seen in anyone outside Rick and myself, he eventually touched the frog. I was surprised that he didn't grab him as other boys would do but seemed very satisfied just to touch him. As the frog jumped wildly back to the safety of the water beneath the lily pads, the boy slowly sat up and looked around. I could tell now that the boy was far more aware than most other people. Faint movement caught his eye, he seemed to sense things moving outside his senses, and he appeared captivated by all that was going on around him.

I was excited and delighted to see that in another person other than Rick and Grandfather. Most people I found in the woods seemed to be traveling in a fog, totally unaware of all that was going on around them. People didn't move with the flow of the woods and were rather clumsy, removed from the Earth in an obvious sort of way. Wilderness to most people was something to be passed through or conquered, never something that was part of them. I found that when most people went into the woods, they missed everything, especially the deeper spiritual truths. This boy was different, attuned, and totally engrossed in the Earth. He would be a perfect candidate for Grandfather to teach, and potentially another rare friend to talk to. My heart was beyond excitement about meeting this new friend. Just as I was going to get up and introduce myself, a man walked to the far edge of the pond and began to search its edge with his eyes.

"Trying to get out of work again!" the man said viciously as the boy stood at rapt attention. "Always going off to this pond, always playing with the animals, always dreaming,'' the man shouted, now walking toward the boy in a threatening manner. The boy was visibly shaken, cowering to the upper edge of the bank as the man approached. All I could hear was the man yelling at the boy as they walked off. The man told the boy that if he slipped away again, he would be beaten. He was tired of the chores not being done, tired of the boy going off into the woods, and tired of the way the boy talked to ''stupid animals.'' He screamed at the boy that he would never be able to make it in the world without hard work. Running away to the woods would get him nowhere. As they walked, a hawk screamed, the boy turned to look at the sky, and the father punched him to the ground. Dragging the boy and screaming, the man walked back to the house.

I was upset and angry. Certainly I knew that some people got in trouble for going into the woods, but they were never so viciously attacked, physically and verbally. This boy showed such great potential and interest, and the man seemed to be trying to beat it out of him. At least my parents were understanding and enjoyed the fact that I went into the woods rather than go to town and hang out with the other kids. My father saw the woods as a source of wisdom and adventure and encouraged me, but this boy had no such luck. Overwhelmed with anger, I stalked around the pond and through the thickets, toward where the man and boy had disappeared. I could smell the barnyard and knew that it was close to where they lived, so I got deeper into the brush and became a shadow again. Edging my way through the thick brush, I came to a barbed-wire fence and pushed my face under so as to get a better view.

I saw the boy again, at the far side of the barnyard, working on the roof of a small outbuilding. His father, as I assumed the man to be, was nowhere to be seen. As I looked around I realized that this was a very strange place.

The wagons, houses, and equipment were old yet looked new. I could see no trucks or cars. In fact, I could see nothing modern at all. At the time it made absolutely no sense to me, and I didn't remember anyplace like this in the Pine Barrens. I passed these thoughts out of my mind as my attention was drawn back to the boy, high up on the roof. Again the hawk had caught his attention, and he was looking skyward, just as his father walked around the edge of the building, carrying an armload of wood. The man screamed up at the boy; startled, the boy jerked around, lost his balance, and fell from the roof, landing upside down with a tremendous thud that I could hear all the way to the fence.

I was horrified, for the boy was surely hurt badly. I took no notice of the activity going on at the outbuilding as I carefully crawled through the pasture and closer to the place where the boy had fallen. It seemed to take forever, my mind swam with disbelief, and an extreme hatred of the man welled up inside me. I edged closer to the building, to a point where I was still concealed but could get a good look at what was going on. I was too frightened of the man to show myself and instinctively thought it better that I remain hidden. I was afraid that if the man saw me, he would beat me as he had the boy. As I pushed my way through the final border of grasses, I could see the boy lying on the ground, ashen-gray, bloody, and unmoving. A woman, probably his mother, sat nearby, clutching his hand, trembling, and sobbing almost uncontrollably. The father stood nearby, looking stunned.

I could hear the father clearly, and in a tone of a remorse mixed with anger he said that the boy was dead. The mother's sobs increased to a wail of grief. Then the father spoke harshly to the mother, saying, ''It's the daydreaming and the woods that killed him. If it weren't for the stupid ani-

mals and the stupid daydreaming, he would still be alive!''
I could take no more, and in a fit of anger and anguish, I
stood up and ran to the father screaming, but they paid no
attention. As I ran toward them my foot caught on a section
of cut log, and I fell hard to the ground. I stood back up
in a rage, all was dark, and I was back in the same place I
had fallen during my trip to the hill.

I was amazed at the intensity and the reality of the dream.
There was no farm, no boy, no father, just a stupid dream.
I felt so shaken, bewildered, and unable to piece together
time, place, dream, and reality. As I lay there the events of
the past day and night began to rush back to me. I remembered that I'd taken a new path to the hill, that I'd exhausted myself pushing through the brush and had fallen.
It all became clear, and now, as the sun rose, the full reality
returned. As I lifted myself from the ground, just a few feet
from my head was the gravestone of the boy that Grandfather had shown to me almost a year before. I was numb
and frightened. As I wandered off to the trail leading to the
hill, I wondered to myself if I had truly seen into the life
of the boy in the grave, or had I just imagined the whole
thing. The reality and possibility of it all troubled me
deeply as I walked to the hill.

I walked on to Prophecy Hill, deep in thought about the
events of the past day. If what I had experienced was a
senseless dream, then why was it affecting me in such a
way, taking over my conscious mind with analysis, almost
haunting me. Grandfather had said that most dreams were
but the mind playing, but those dreams that were very
vivid, very demanding, and that haunted the mind through
the waking hours were sources of wisdom, messages from
the deeper self or the spirit world. He also had said that if
a dream was important, then it would recur frequently until
the dreamer interpreted the message. This, in a big way,

felt like just such a dream, and I began to feel that ending up at the foot of the gravestone had not been just coincidence. Yet there must be more to the dream, for the deeper meaning still seemed to elude me.

Finally reaching the hill, I went about building camp. The making of the debris hut and the fire, finding water and gathering food, got me out of my thoughts for a while, and I was lost to the intensity and excitement of survival. Survival at such a basic level, where one has no equipment or supplies, is such a purification of the mind and spirit. It is always exciting, always an adventure, and is the only way that man can truly become one with the Earth. Survival living is much like a Vision Quest, for it purifies the body and opens the mind. It was during the building of camp that I realized with certainty that it was not coincidence that I had ended up at the gravesite, and that the dream was important to me, though I still did not know why.

Now, as dusk began to approach and the work of the camp was finished, I sat for a long time thinking about the boy in my dream. The primary reasons for the dreams had become apparent and important. Here had been a boy who obviously was captivated by the pure and natural, but that love was beaten and finally destroyed by his father and an enslaving work ethic. Certainly the dream had taken place at a different time, like passing through a spiritual curtain to the past. But the question of how I could be really sure filled my mind and precluded all other thought. For some reason I had to have physical proof of some kind that would confirm that the boy in my dreams really had existed. It was no longer enough just to accept the vague lessons.

I felt drawn to go back to the gravesite that night and try to find where the houses and buildings had stood. Even more important was to find the pond, for if I found it, I could get my bearings and find the other buildings. I knew

that time had probably destroyed them and returned the area
to the Earth, but I felt compelled to find them, anyway—
why, I didn't know. I just had to find that pond, and find
it that night. I knew that it would be difficult, especially in
the dark, but the pond surely must still be there if the dream
had been real. The draw to find the pond was so strong that
it drove me from the hill. There could be no waiting for
morning light.

I was terrified as I walked to the old graveyard. I had
never truly been frightened in the world of creation, for
wilderness was always home, but I was at times frightened
of the spirit world. That world was always so over-
whelming and so powerful. In the wilderness I could take
care of myself, for the Earth provided everything I needed,
especially purity of thought and security. I knew where all
things were in Nature, and I knew that I was part of it all.
But in the spirit world I was a child. There was so much
to understand, so much unknown, and much of the unknown was very frightening at times. Then again, what I
was learning now was survival in the spirit world, and
someday I hoped to feel as comfortable there.

The trip to the graveyard seemed to take forever, as my
fear at times overwhelmed me. But my heart seemed to
drag me on, until I finally arrived at the gravestone I sought.
I could barely see its outline in the dark, but I knew that it
was the right stone, for it was nearly fully covered with
vines, like none of the others. I sat down for a while, to
rest and to sort out my thoughts, trying to decide which
way to go first in my search for the pond. I remembered
that Grandfather had so often told us to follow our "inner
Vision" instead of our minds, for the following of our inner
Vision would never be wrong. With that I began to wander
around the landscape, guided by inner feelings rather than
conscious ones, and I found myself drawn to the far end of

the graveyard. Not a logical choice because it was uphill, and a pond would never be located there. It was then that I heard the croak of a frog, followed by a distinctive splash.

I ran in the direction of the sound and within a few moments came to the edge of the pond. It was located uphill from the graveyard but deceptively hidden in a hollow between two small hills. That is why it wasn't obvious to me before, for it was located in a place that one would not expect to find water. If I had followed my logical mind, I never would have found it, but by following my heart I was led right to its edge. It was definitely the same pond I had seen in my dreams, and though it was very overgrown around its edges, it was still the same odd shape that I remembered. I was at once delighted and in awe that I had found it, for it confirmed that I must have been there in my dreams and not in this time.

I reoriented myself to the side of the pond that I had approached in my dream. It was easy to see the exact place where the boy had stalked the frog, for the shoreline had not changed. Retracing my steps, I headed to the far end of the pond and headed in the general direction of where the buildings had been seen in my dreams. The field had now overgrown, and once leaving the pond, I had no way of judging distance or the exact location. Again I went mostly on instinct and inner Vision, being guided solely by my feelings. The original fear had now vanished, for I was too excited about finding the pond and confirming my dream. I was still confused as to why, and how it was important to me in my life. Surely I had not been driven out of the woods by my parents, only encouraged, and my life was not even similar to the boy in my dream.

I continued wandering and searching the area but with no luck. My heart and feelings told me that I was there, but I could find no evidence of any buildings. I felt tormented in a way, tormented by something, a feeling or emotion that kept nagging at my heart. As I walked on, the feelings intensified, and for some unknown reason I grew very cautious. Within the next few steps my caution was justified. When I kicked the ground to find evidence of a structure, I dislodged some small stones, which rolled ahead, echoed down some unseen shaft, and splashed into water. I had found a well. Crawling now on hands and knees, I found the lip of the well in the darkness, and dropping stones, I determined it to be only about ten feet deep. I realized then that if I hadn't been traveling in the heart, I would have gone down the well, which was right in my path.

As I sat at the well's edge I looked up into the distant sky, trying again to orient myself to the pond, the graveyard, and to the general direction of Prophecy Hill. It was then that I noticed the remains of an old chimney, reaching like a solitary spire to the sky. It was partially decomposed and parts of it had fallen, yet it was still tall, reaching almost two stories. Obviously I had found the place where the house had once stood, and I approached the chimney with caution. In the dark there could have been all manner of debris or holes that could make going dangerous, and I didn't want to take a chance after the near accident at the well. As I neared the chimney I sat down on its edge to rest, thoroughly satisfied that my dream had been reality.

I knew very well that it was quite common to slip through spiritual reality and into the past, for the spirit world knows no time and place. The big question was still the reason I was given the dream, and why it was important to me. I realized that many times a dream, like a Vision, had to be interpreted, and that it sometimes took years. However, I also knew that I was driven to this place, and to the hill, and as yet did not know why. All I knew was that I had to follow my heart, for to deny that inner Vision, one denies any possibility of an answer. As I slipped deeper into thought I could feel a sense of wonder, laced with an innate and deep anticipation, though nothing seemed to be around, not even in spirit.

I felt myself slipping in and out of sleep, going from reality to dream and back to reality again. I was extremely exhausted from the long trip, the ordeal of the previous night, making camp, and now searching for the old homestead. I wanted to fight sleep, for I wanted answers in a real way, not again from a dream or from a feeling. Finally sleep won the battle, and I gave in, feeling that I would do better to explore the old homestead in the morning. I remember being upset with myself and my inability to stay awake. I felt that someone like Grandfather would have stayed awake and found energy where there was none to be had. He would have transcended his physical self, as all searchers must learn to do. What I didn't realize at the time was that my heart was telling me to sleep, not my mind.

I awoke to a brilliantly clear and beautiful morning. Birds were in grand voice, and the whole of creation seemed refreshed, beautiful, and very alive. I was thoroughly rested and my mind was clear. My sleep had been virtually dreamless, yet I had the feeling that I knew something, something very deeply spiritual, something that would change the way I saw life. It felt like all at once I had all the answers, but then, as I tried to logically sort things out, I knew absolutely nothing. I did know that something had definitely changed inside me in a very dramatic way. I left the homestead after a little exploration and returned to the hill, for the hill was still compelling me to stay there for a while. Though I thought that I had resolved the dream of the boy, I still had to find out why I was still drawn to the hill.

I spent the remainder of the day exploring the hill. My

mind still remained clear, and I rarely thought about the dream or of the prophecies Grandfather had given to me on that hill. I searched the area around the hill and found that it was not far from the site of the homestead. I had gone the long way around in the past, and now I knew that it was easier to get there by just going down the far side of the hill. Surely the occupants of the homestead must have known about the hill, for parts of an old footpath still led up to it from the homestead side. The path was worn into the Earth, much like the ancient Native American migration paths still visible in various parts of the woods. I was delighted to find a connection from my dream about the boy and the homestead to the top of the hill, though I did not know if that connection held any message for me.

As dusk entered the woods I went to the far edge of the hill to pray and meditate, a practice we followed every evening and morning whenever possible. It helped us sort out Grandfather's many lessons of Nature, and reflect on all the things we had accomplished that day. It also gave us much-needed time for worship and to talk to the Creator. As I sat watching the sun set, deep in prayer, I again got a feeling that something was watching me. It was the same over-whelming feeling that I had had during the night that Grandfather had told us of the four prophecies. This time the feeling was more intense and more frightening. It was the kind of feeling I would get whenever I suspected wild dogs were around, but did not know exactly where they were. The feeling never passed but intensified to a point where I could concentrate on nothing else but the feeling. Yet there was nothing out of place on the landscape, and the flow of Nature was still and calm.

As it grew fully dark, the feeling became so over-whelming that I had to get back to camp and light a fire. I needed the security of camp to try to get my mind on other

things and away from the feeling of being closely scrutinized. Yet even in camp, with the security and the light of
the fire, I still felt some threatening presence watching me,
in essence stalking me. Again there was nothing tangible
that foretold of this stalker, nothing out of place in Nature,
just a deep inner feeling that was especially important in
communication with the spiritual world, and I assumed that
this thing that watched me was from that world. Especially
because there were no physical signs of any threatening
presence.

It was then, in the frail security of camp, that I heard a
distinct noise in the distant brush. Whatever it was that
watched me, that stalked me, spirit or reality, it now was
making itself manifest. At first I thought it could be a rogue
dog out searching for food, but the sound of the footfalls
were definitely that of man. The quality of the sound, however, was very light and a bit draggy, possibly someone
injured. The steps, though fumbling, moved steadily closer,
until they finally stopped in the thicket just outside of the
firelight. I was terrified, unable to move, and clear thinking
became impossible. All manner of thoughts raced through
my head in a blur as to what this thing, this man, could
possibly be. I was definitely too far out in the woods for it
to be just a casual wanderer, for even the hardiest hunter
of the Pine Barrens rarely ventured this far from the road.

For a very long time there was no other sound. The surrounding woods were strangely silent and unmoving, almost as if waiting for something to happen. My heart felt
like it was going to jump through my throat. Then finally
a voice called to me from the thicket, a boy's voice, the
same voice I had heard talking to the frog in my dream.
Without waiting for a response from me, the boy spoke
again, saying, ''I was kept from my dream, from living and
exploring Nature by my father and his work ethic. I gave

in to him reluctantly and abandoned all the things I loved. We all have things that remove us from our path of dreams and Visions. My death was from an overbearing father who would not accept my dreams and Visions, and what, then, will yours be? What will try to drive you from your path, from your woods, from your love? It can be many things, from fathers and families, to the unwritten codes of society, to the many things we have to do to stay alive.''

The voice continued. ''You have wondered how your life and my life have come together in a dream, and you think that we are not similar. My life came to an early end because I gave in to things I did not believe in. Someday you will face the same decisions, but I warn you that they will not be as obvious as my father and family for there will be many subtle things you must face. If I had continued along my path of love, who knows what I could have done to save the Earth and possibly even my family? What will you do to follow your Vision? Will your life end in some forgotten grave, in some forgotten homestead, never to make a difference? So then, learn from me so that my life is not wasted, and never let anything stand in the path of your Vision.'' With those words the voice stopped before I could speak, and Nature returned to its natural flow.

I looked away from the distant brush, where the voice had come. Gazing back into the fire, shaken and upset, my thoughts were in a whirl. It all happened so quickly and without warning that I felt shocked. In fact, I did not know if it had been spiritual reality or just another dream. However, the words hit me hard because they were so urgent and so true. I knew that somehow the spirit of that boy had given me a profound warning. Whether it had been a dream or reality did not make a difference. As I thought about his words I could see for the first time how our lives were momentarily connected and similar. Someday I would have to face the same ridicule and anger that he had once faced, and I hoped that the encounter would not end in death. Whether it was physical or spiritual death made no difference.

Again I was shocked away from the fire of my thoughts as I heard footfalls, and Grandfather walked into camp. He sat down across the fire from me and looked into my eyes for a long time. I know that he could see the tension of the moment and the swirling of questions in my head. He smiled and said, "Take heed of the child's warning, for if you falter from your path, your dreams and Visions, you will surely die, if not spiritually then physically. For a man not living his heart is living death. Your tests will be strong, and you must be strong, for that is the only way you can affect the spirit-that-moves-in-all-things. You must work beyond the self, following your Vision, or perish doing nothing to change the path of man. You will become that boy." He then simply walked away into the night, leaving me still confused but closer to understanding.

I stayed at the hill for the next two days, trying to sort out the meaning of all the dreams and words. Certainly there was nothing in my life now to drive me from the woods or from my Visions, but I knew that it would not be the same in the distant future. At least now I was on-guard that something could slip into my life and drive me from my path. I did not know when, but I would be ready for it, or so I hoped. No matter what I thought, the spirit of the boy was sent to me for a reason, and I had to heed his warning. My life was forever intertwined with that once forgotten boy in that once forgotten grave. Now he will never be forgotten, and he was finally making a difference.

3

The Demon
of Distraction

It was a long and bitter-cold walk from the camp area to the distant stream. Snow had covered the ground in a thick blanket, small pines bowed toward the ground, unable to hold up their heavy burdens of white. Even though the snow had stopped and the sky was clear, a bitter wind still swept across the snow, and all of creation seemed to be hiding from the cold. With a full moon glistening off the snowbanks, fields, and bowing trees, the landscape appeared surrealistic, mysterious, and filled with hidden adventures. The silence was profound, even the powerful wind was muffled, and all I could really hear was the sound of my heavy breathing as we walked toward the distant water. Grandfather walked up ahead, barely visible as the blowing snow encircled him, and Rick walked somewhere behind me, though out of sight. The swirling snow entombed each of us so that we walked alone.

By the time we reached the edge of the stream I was numb but still able to get a fire started quickly. Grandfather remained absolutely quiet, without expression, giving no hints as to what we were doing there or why. Rick solemnly helped me build the fire and collect some brush to sit upon, both of us anxiously awaiting the moment that Grandfather would speak.

At this point Rick and I could only guess why we were there. Several hours earlier we had been sitting back at camp, talking to Grandfather about body control and how the mind could control the body fully. We had learned from Grandfather how to slow our heart rate to about twenty beats per minute, and then in the flash of an eye to elevate it to over one hundred and seventy beats per minute, all while sitting perfectly still. We had learned to slow blood flow or stop the flow of blood gushing from a wound altogether, and we had learned to shorten the duration of a common cold. We could use our minds to push us farther and harder than we could ever do physically, and we could call upon the primal mind to help us survive in dangerous situations, where the power of the animal within was needed.

But, I suspected, the lessons about to be encountered this night would take us deeper into body and mind control. Certainly we had learned so many things in the control of body through the mind, thought, and belief, but we still had not mastered it to perfection. The harsh winds and bitter cold of this night made us nervous with anticipation.

To Grandfather the control of body was important for two reasons. If we were to learn and live as ''one'' with the Earth, then body control would help us do many of the things that most untrained people could not do. Body control would help us work efficiently in extreme weather conditions, and would enable us to go without water and food for long periods of time by conserving, internally, what food we had consumed. It would help us find an almost unlimited supply of energy in times of need, heal wounds at a faster rate, drive off infection, and otherwise function at optimum levels of strength, no matter what we faced. It would allow us to travel greater distances, limit our rest periods, or make them unnecessary, and it would allow us to go into places where most men would fear to go. Grandfather told us that body control was used by the ancient scouts when they had to travel across rugged landscapes or deserts. They would emerge easily from these harsh environments, hardly the worse for wear.

The mind's ability to control the body was even more important for spiritual quests. So many spiritual endeavors, such as Vision Questing or Vision Walking, ceremony, and the art of spiritual healings, take far more strength and discipline than anything we would encounter in survival, tracking, and the study of awareness. The pursuit of spiritual things demanded an absolute concentration. A concentration that could not be broken by anything the body might be going through at the time. To be bothered by cold winds or hot deserts during the time of prayer or spiritual questing would only remove us from that prayer or that spiritual quest. If we were concerned about the body, pain, or discomfort, then we would be distracted and thus never be fully involved in what we wanted to accomplish. This partial involvement would then negate the effort and we would get poor results.

This was the law; the body, and the mind, had to be mastered, not only in the things of survival but more so for the quests of the spirit. Grandfather considered body control to be the "doorway to the soul," for it was through body control that we learn to tap into everything else. Thus body and mind control, which Grandfather called "fusion of self," was an ongoing lesson. There was rarely a day that passed that this fusion of self was not mentioned, or something new not added to what we already knew. This day, we felt, would be no exception.

We sat for a long time by the edge of the water, warming ourselves by the fire. Grandfather still remained mute and stoic, away from the warmth, as if to show us that the fire was not needed and that he had more important things to do. At the time I felt like I was taking the easy way out, but then a survivalist uses whatever he needs to survive. Still, I felt like a child that needed to be warmed before I could enjoy anything pure, natural, and cold. Grandfather finally spoke, saying, "This fire has become your crutch, your doorway, for without it you would not enjoy fully the purity of this wilderness and the storm. Not only can you not fully enjoy, but you must take this excess baggage with you, thus restricting and confining your body. Through control you must learn to wean yourself from these shackles and walk free."

With those words Grandfather wandered off into the storm, leaving Rick and me to nurse our thoughts and the fire. I tried to wander off into the snowy landscape and explore but frequently I had to return to the fire for warmth. Long ago I had beaten the type of cold that would drive most people from the woods by learning to give in to it and allow its energy to flow through me. But this storm was too cold and violent, and surely I would freeze to death without the fire. I still felt defeated in a big way, since Grandfather had gone off for hours with less clothing on than we had, and he wasn't even back yet. I, on the other hand, had been back to the prison of the fire several times. I could not fully explore the winter landscape, because the cold had driven me away each time.

In a way I felt sorry for myself, defeated, and imprisoned by my need for the fire. I so desperately wanted to do what Grandfather was doing, wandering about the snowy cold landscape, free and unrestricted, to do and go wherever he chose. I felt as if I were missing everything, that the snowy woods was passing me by and I would never know its secrets. I felt so cheated, cheated by my own body and mind and by my inability to travel very far from the fire for very long. I tried to use what little body control I knew, but each time I tried, my mind was torn away by the cold winds and driving snow. I failed again and again, to the point of despair and anger.

Grandfather finally returned to camp and sat down near the fire. He looked absolutely unaffected by the cold night and certainly didn't need the warmth of the fire. I knew that he had seen so much and probably had explored areas that I would never again have the chance to explore. I told him how upset I was that I could not leave the fire for very long and that I had to constantly walk while out of camp and never sit for very long, because the cold bit through me and drove me back to the fire. In fact, I could not concentrate on the purity of the night, only on fighting the cold.

Grandfather remained silent as he listened to my plight. I knew that he knew exactly what I was feeling, and I also suspect that he had all the answers. Finally he said, ''You give the storm, the cold, and the night far too much power. You believe that you are cold, and so you will be cold. You fear the storm and the wind, and the storm then becomes your enemy. So, then, remove the power from the storm and it will lose its hold on you. Allow the storm to flow through you and do not fight it, and it will become your power. Do as you once learned to do at the Medicine Cabin, when you ran through the snow naked and finally learned not to fight Nature.''

My mind immediately raced back to the night at the Medicine Cabin when Grandfather had us run home through a similar storm. Certainly that night we had learned a valuable lesson of not resisting Nature but allowing the storm to flow through us, thus we were not cold when we got home. We had fought the storm the entire way, feeling the snow and wind bite through our bare flesh to a point of pain, but we somehow had learned not to resist the storm, and suddenly we were no longer cold. But that had been a mild storm compared to this one; there was no way we could do the same thing now. Temperatures were far colder and the storm more violent, and to give in to the storm would only kill us.

Grandfather spoke again, as usual knowing what questions were racing through my mind. He said, "This is not the mild storm that you knew at the Medicine Cabin, and it cannot be transcended by merely giving in to its power. What you must learn to do is teach your mind to control your body, uplifting its burning energy so that the cold is no longer something to be feared and fought. Remember, however, that if you uplift your energy now, then you must replace that energy later. The way to rise above this storm and your flesh, then, is to command the body to do so. Concentrate on and believe what is desired, and the power will be given to you.

"You have learned to deal with some storms, cold, and oppressive heat, by not resisting those forces but becoming one with them. Now you must learn to deal with the flesh by commanding the body to ignore the storm and burn away the cold with its own energy. Once mastered, you will then learn to transcend the cold through the spiritual self, where there is no need to make the body suffer, for through the spirit there is no cold, no heat, no discomfort. Thus spirit, blends, and becomes one with spirit, then there is no separation between your spirit and the spirit of the storm. Until then, until you learn to transcend the cold through the spirit, then you must master your body through your mind.

"Now," he said, "put out the fire, remove your clothes, and enter the water."

His words stabbed through my mind as I looked up at him abruptly, in utter disbelief. Surely he must be kidding, I thought, for to break through the ice and into the water would certainly mean our deaths. Looking at Grandfather's expression, I knew that he wasn't kidding, so without question I began to remove my clothes. As Rick and I undressed, Grandfather instructed us, as he had so many other times when using our body control. He said, "You must give the water and the cold no power over you. You must concentrate fully and completely to bring your energy from the center of your body and move it to its limits. There must be no doubt in your mind, only absolute belief, unwavering faith, in that which you will do."

I concentrated very hard on sending my core energy throughout my body; I began to perspire, even though I stood at the water's edge. As the first drops of sweat appeared on my forehead, my confidence and belief grew stronger, and I entered the water. As I walked, the waters felt warm, thin ice easily breaking away, but as I got deeper, my mind floundered, thinking about the ice, the water, and the cold winds. I began to feel the cold rushing into my body, making my mind falter even more. The cold stabbed and tore at my flesh, the wind that hit my head seemed to make it swoon with an uncontrollable pain. I had finally reached the point of such intense pain and fear that I was about to run from the water and back to the fire. Grandfather's voice broke that fear; he simply said, "Concentrate."

I fought the fear and the intensity of the cold, concentrating again on what I was trying to do. I forced my mind back to bring up my deepest energy. It was difficult at first, but then I finally felt my body warming and the cold water losing its sting. I began to grow more comfortable, almost warm, and then my concentration was again broken by the sound of the winds and the rattle of ice on the turbulent waters. I suddenly lost it altogether, and had to rush back to the land, where Grandfather had a fire blazing. Rick was already standing there, but I felt so defeated, so much like a failure, for I so desperately wanted to learn what Grandfather was trying to teach.

After we warmed ourselves and got dressed, Grandfather finally talked to us about what we had tried but failed to do. There was no disappointment in his voice, no accusations, just a warmth that said he had been where we are at one time in his life. "As you have seen, it is not enough to allow the cold to flow through you, nor should you fight that cold," he said. "What is important is that the body must respond to the commands and beliefs of the mind. The mind must have absolute concentration, which empowers the belief, which then empowers the body to do that which is desired. It is as I have taught you before, though now we want the body to do a specific task, not something that is general and simple. This will take complete concentration, not only on what is desired but also on what the body must do to produce what is desired."

Grandfather did not speak for a while but allowed us to digest what he had said. Finally he continued, "So it is not enough merely to allow the storm and the cold to flow through you, nor is it enough to remove the storm's power over you. These things will work many times, but this time, with the intensity of this cold, there must be more, much more. There must be so strong a belief in the mind that nothing can influence its power. That belief must then be sent to the body, and the body must then respond with that which is desired. Afterward the body must have time to replenish and rest, the energy must then be replaced. What is most important is that the absolute concentration must not be broken.

"This concentration is that which empowers the belief, which empowers the body," he continued. "Now you will understand why I say so often that the most powerful demon is that of distraction, followed by the demon of self-doubt." As he spoke, I imagined all the most hideous demons I had ever encountered, both in imagination and reality. Now, for the first time, I understood what Grandfather had meant so often when he spoke of the demon of distraction, for I could see how powerful it could become. This night it defeated me, humiliated me, and kept me from learning a powerful lesson. I had been beaten by that demon so many times before, but this night I finally learned its name.

"Your concentration was broken when you were distracted by the cold and the wind," Grandfather then said. "Once your concentration was broken, so was your belief, and your body faltered and finally succumbed to the cold. What you then must do is practice absolute concentration, free of all distraction."

"But how do I deal with this distraction?" I asked. Grandfather answered, saying, "You will learn to deal with the demon three different ways. Sometimes you must aggressively fight that demon, sometimes you must confront that demon, and sometimes you must passively accept that demon. Each time, each situation, then, is new and different. Each time the demon of distraction must be overcome in its own way, unique unto that situation."

"But how will I know how, when, and what to use to conquer that demon?" I asked. Grandfather continued, "Many times, such as dealing with fear, which is an ugly and powerful distraction, we must confront that fear for it to be banished. Other times we must use aggressive force, such as when we are in a dire survival situation. The demon must be beaten back with a brutal aggression. Most times we need only passively accept and identify that demon and it will lose its power. But at no time can we give that demon of distraction or self-doubt any power, for it feeds upon the power we add unto it, and with each cycle it grows more powerful.''

''How do I practice this absolute concentration?'' I then asked.

After a long and thoughtful moment Grandfather spoke again, saying, ''You practice this concentration through control of the body and mind, which eventually leads to the greatest control: that of spirit. But to have absolute concentration and control you must be totally committed to the task at hand and thoroughly absorbed in its outcome, so that there is no room for anything else. This is accomplished with little steps, small successes, each growing stronger and leading to greater success. What you have tried to do tonight is a great success, because you touched what could be. Now you must work to create a complete success, but that will take commitment and hard work.''

Throughout the next year both Rick and I worked at being able to concentrate fully, without any distraction. At first it was difficult, for our minds wandered, our meditations broke, and we would fail. But little by little we were able to overcome so many of the distractions that had so often defeated us in the past. We started off with little challenges, such as sitting for long periods of time, concentrating on something on the landscape, transforming that entity into a type of mandala. Each time a distraction threatened to take us from our meditation we would fight it, confront it, or passively recognize it, thus effectively destroying its power and energy.

Sometimes the distraction was difficult to defeat; other times it went away quickly; and there were times that we had to try all the methods, until one finally worked. The problem, at times, was that the act of defeating a distraction would in itself become a distraction, and then the act of defeating that would become another distraction. This became very frustrating because we began to replace one distraction with another. What we were trying to seek was a purity in our struggle, where the act of confronting and defeating a distraction became second nature and would not remove us from that which we wanted to accomplish. What we didn't realize is that by seeking this purity we were touching the spiritual fusion of which Grandfather so often spoke.

As the year moved on and the incident at the cold waters became a distant memory, we became more involved in defeating more intense distractions. We put ourselves into situations where we needed absolute body and mind control in order to succeed, where the slightest distraction would cause instant failure. We practiced pushing our limits physically and mentally, where once involved, nothing short of an explosion would tear our minds away. Our ability grew with each step, yet we were such a long way from accomplishing such control as would be needed to enter water and sweat during a severe winter storm. We had mastered many of the small distractions but still hadn't made many breakthroughs into the grander realms.

It seemed that whenever we undertook something that would require more concentration and specific demands, we would be beaten by the demon of distraction and self-doubt. We failed all of our grand attempts at control without distraction, though we still had many little triumphs. We could not get over the final hurdle, the wall that kept us from touching the things Grandfather wanted us to do. With now the better part of a year having passed since we tried to enter the cold waters, I still felt like a failure and still struggled, despite frequent small triumphs. Finally the day came when I broke through the wall to savor a tremendous victory.

It was winter again, nearly a full year since we had attempted and failed to enter the frigid waters. Rick and I were camped one snowy weekend near a small frozen lake in the center of the Pine Barrens. The winter up to this point in the year had been quite mild, rarely getting below freezing. But this week we had been hit by small storms, subfreezing temperatures, and a continuous flow of cold winds. The landscape was particularly quiet, as animals rarely ventured out past the thickets and into the winds. However, it afforded Rick and me a tremendous opportunity for exploration, as most of the swamps and sphagnum bogs had frozen over, and we could easily walk their surfaces.

During the second day of our stay we both went our separate ways to explore. The winds were more intense that day, and the temperature was in the low teens, yet the cold held no power over us because the sun was shining strong and the thickets protected us from the wind. I was gone for much of the day, tracking along the interior streams that capillaried through the large swamp near our camp. I only began my return trip after dusk, arriving back at camp by moonlight. I had assumed that Rick would be back at camp when I arrived, as he was only exploring the edge of the lake, but when I returned, he was not there.

I started a fire and awaited his return, but after about an hour I began to grow worried and went down to the lake to search for him, though I did not feel that anything was wrong. Arriving at the lake, I was taken back by the most spectacular view of the day. The moon glistened off the ice, turning the lake into a wonderland. It was so bright and intense that I actually had to squint, and I was so captivated by its beauty that I hardly noticed the cold, biting winds. As I gazed in awe across the lake I was startled to see a figure walking toward me on the ice. It was Rick, returning from his hike.

As I watched him approach, it finally dawned on me that he was walking on the lake. I panicked because I knew that the ice at the center of the lake was dangerously thin and would in no way support any weight. I had found this out earlier in the day when I attempted to walk a few feet out and fell through. Rick was out there and certainly was not aware of the thin ice. I yelled to him but he didn't respond, for the wind muffled my voice. I ran to the edge and screamed at the top of my voice, waving my arms. I could see Rick look toward me, wave, then plunge through the ice and disappear.

I went into a blind panic. Without thought I crashed onto the ice and broke through to my waist. I struggled forward, breaking ice as I went. Though I could see Rick's head and knew that he still was not under the water, I plainly saw that he was floundering. The surrounding ice had imprisoned him and he could not get back up onto thicker ice. I pressed on like a raging animal, sometimes swimming but most of the time breaking the ice that lay before me, creating a clear path from Rick to the shore. I noticed, too, that Rick was beginning to do the same thing, edging slowly toward me.

We called to each other as we drew closer, our voices barely audible above the screaming winds. I continued breaking ice and intermittently swimming, fearing all the time that I would not get to Rick in time. I had traveled well over one hundred yards and had cut a rather large path through the thin ice, and now all I had to do was connect that path to Rick and we would be able to make it back to shore. My head rushed with a thousand whirling thoughts, and all I could clearly remember in my struggle was that I hoped I could get a fire going when we got back to camp.

With one huge shove I broke through to Rick's path, expecting to find him near death. Instead, what I saw literally shocked me to an absolute stop. Rick, instead of being in a blind panic, was laughing and playing as he broke away some of the ice. I suddenly realized that Rick had broken through the wall of self, the demon of distraction, and I was overjoyed at his obvious success. Rick began to shout at me, "We did it! We did it!" And in a dumbfounded sort of a way I realized that I, too, did not feel the cold, the winds, or my own fatigue. I was pouring in sweat and swimming playfully, as if it were a warm summer afternoon.

I had finally transcended the demon of distraction in a big way. I had fought it, beaten it, and had gone beyond the wall that had for so long stood in my way. I felt no cold, no pain, just an exhilaration and energy that caused me to find the ultimate freedom from physical self, from physical and mental limitations. We both swam to shore slowly, talking and playing as we went. Nothing broke our concentration or purpose, for we had transcended the demon of distraction and, ultimately, self-doubt. We walked back to camp, built a warm fire, ate a hearty dinner, and relaxed for a long while, replacing the energy we had burned and reveling in our victory.

We talked and rejoiced for hours, feeling no side effects from our ordeal, other than a deep fatigue that indicated that we had drained ourselves. We had commanded our minds with a powerful belief, and our bodies had responded, never faltering. Our concentration had been so absolute that there had been nothing else in our world other than the water and the safety of each other. All else had been set aside, and in doing so we had set our minds and spirits free. Several other times that night we went back down to the lake to swim, play, sweat, and reaffirm our victory. We played so hard that we finally nearly burned ourselves out, collapsing into the debris huts and into deep and profound sleep—a sleep of triumph and personal victory, for we had bridged the last obstacle.

We awoke to the crackle and hiss of a warm fire. Grandfather had come to our camp early. Before we could utter a word about our adventure and subsequent victory, Grandfather immediately related to us what had happened. As usual we were amazed at how much he knew, even the details of our deepest thoughts. It was almost as if he had been there with us or had somehow helped us in our quest. He said, "You have found the answer, and the answer has found you. Your concentration was so absolute, so pure, that there was no room for distraction or failure. Your goal was more important to you than anything else, and thus you were able to transcend your normal limitations and touch the spirit of absolute freedom.

"You first learned that ultimate control was through fusion of body, mind, and spirit, into a oneness. Thus you were able to transcend most limitations. Then you learned not to give power to problems and that you had a 'choice' as to how to deal with any problem. And now you have learned to command the body through the belief of the mind, through absolute and pure concentration and by transcending distraction. You have learned to rise above that distraction through facing it, fighting it, and through passive recognition, and you have won the first battle, the battle of self-doubt.

"This wisdom," Grandfather said, "that you now possess can be used in survival, to rise above adverse conditions or to command the body to go beyond your own limitations. It can be used in tracking and in the awareness that takes you beyond limits of physical possibility. And it can be used for spiritual enlightenment, so that the spirit can be set free, unencumbered by the body. But most of all it can be used in the world outside the reality of the wilderness, where you have to face the many distractions of man. It will keep you on your path, close to your vision, and living the philosophy of the Earth, when all around you is in chaos. It is a way to transcend the trappings and distractions of man and seek out spiritual paths in the face of all adversity.

"However," Grandfather went on, "the rush and distraction of society and man's world are far more powerful than those demons you will meet in the cold waters or in any wilderness. These demons of distraction come silently, through complacency, invading all parts of your life, and you must always be on-guard. They are not obvious or easily dispelled, like those you have faced in the past, and unlike the intermittent battles you face with these demons in the wilderness, the battles in man's world are constant and relentless. There is no rest, for to rest is to die."

My mind began to rush over all the things that I had encountered in my world outside of the wilderness. School, my limited social life, my family, homework, chores, and the many other things that invaded the wilderness mind, finally could be conquered. I finally had a way to begin to bring the wilderness back out into the world I had to live in and face every day. Though I was only going into the fifth grade at the time, I could feel the demons of society trying to pull me into complacency. I finally had a weapon, a power, that would defeat those demons.

Grandfather spoke again, jarring me from my deep thought. "Now you must learn the ultimate power of freedom and control. It is the power of spiritual fusion, where your spirit and the spirit of the elements, the task, and even the demon of distraction become as one. Then there is no struggle, no need to confront, to fight, or to be passive, for there can be only purity. All things then become possible, for in spiritual fusion there can be no separation of self, no inner or outer dimension, just an absolute oneness with all things."

Today I find that the greatest threat to a spiritual life, especially when lived within the confines of society, is the demon of distraction. It invades all aspects of our existence and enters our lives in a subtle yet powerful way. It breeds a certain complacency, self-doubt, and spiritual limitation. As Grandfather taught, the only way to defeat that demon is to be aware, to concentrate, and never to lose sight of your Vision, for all else is a living death.

4

Fusion of Spirit

We had learned the fusion of self, where the body, mind, and spirit became as one. This was an important step for us because through that fusion we learned to control our bodies through our mind, and control our mind through our spirit. Once fusion of self was achieved, we could touch the primal mind, all the instinct bestowed upon us by the Creator, and we could communicate with the spirit-that-moves-in-all-things through the inner Vision. This could be only attained when all parts of self were whole. But this was not enough, for as we practiced, we found that there was something missing, something Grandfather had purposely left out. I suspect that it had been because first he expected mastery of the basic fusion.

It took time to understand all the concepts and application of this "fusion." We realized that it was a passageway to the greater self. Fusion was a way to get out of the island prison of ego and logical thought, and to expand into the force, the spirit-that-moves-in-all-things. We had practiced

this fusion first through attempting to control the function
of the body through the absolute belief of the mind. We
pushed beyond our limits of physical endurance and began
to accomplish things that would normally be impossible.
We learned to release the primal mind and that animal that
dwells within us all, and to use it in extreme and dangerous
survival situations. Most of all, we practiced controlling our
minds through the desires of the spirit and were able to
touch the spirit-that-moves-in-all-things.

We did feel a limitation to this fusion of self, not at first
but as we grew older and could sense a world beyond the
force of life. We knew that there had to be more, for we
could see that in Grandfather's words and actions. There
was something beyond that fusion of self, something that
would take us well beyond all physical limitations. Our
feelings about this world beyond were confirmed when
Grandfather alluded to the "fusion of spirit" while we were
attempting an extreme body-control exercise in frigid winter waters. He had said that after we mastered fusion of the
self we could then master the fusion of spirit, which was
what he called the "absolute oneness."

That year we spent trying to break through the barriers
of mind, until we could enter frigid waters with such belief
and body control that we would sweat. This became a turning point in our lives and in Grandfather's teachings. It was
then that Grandfather began to teach us the fusion of spirit
and the absolute oneness. The first teachings began on a
self-imposed forced march that Rick and I were taking, to
push the limits of our minds' ability to control our body.
During that walk, at the point of failure, Grandfather began
to teach us to go beyond what we knew and to tap into a
greater power.

We had heard from Grandfather that the Apache scouts
could travel hundreds of miles across the most difficult

landscapes and in the most hideous weather conditions, without rest, food, or water. He said that this was done by mind and spirit, more than body, and enabled the scout to go where few men would dare to go. Rick and I, of course, were intrigued by the prospects and decided to create a trek of our own. While still in the fall season we planned a winter hike from the Medicine Cabin to Cape May. It would be a trip of over one hundred miles through the winding trails of the Pine Barrens. We would take no equipment, food, or water, and attempt to do the trip nonstop. Though we had done the trip before, it had taken us nearly four days and three camps, and it was in the mild summer season. A nonstop winter trip would be a brutal challenge.

It was the beginning of January and we were still on Christmas break when we began our winter trek to Cape May. Winds were strong all week and the cold nearly killing. Snows had fallen periodically, but they hardly covered the ground. The winter sky seemed to pour out its wrath on the landscape, making the animals seek constant cover. We had decided to wear as little clothing during the hike as possible, only shirt, pants, and moccasins. No other equipment was taken, for we wanted to do exactly as the ancient scouts had done. The more of a challenge we could make the trip, the more difficult the journey, the more we would learn.

Grandfather seemed excited that we would try to make the journey. I suspect that he knew it would be good for us to put to the ultimate test what we had practiced for so long. The night before we left, he sat us down and began to talk about our trip. He also wanted to advise us about what to be careful of along the way, both physically and spiritually. I could tell that he knew what would happen; what we would go through physically and mentally; and how very close we would come to our limits. He began by telling us the reason the scouts undertook such treks and what they would ultimately teach.

Grandfather said, "The scouts needed to control their bodies with precision, for the scout was required to do what others could not do. The scout had to travel long distances, going without sleep, food, and even water for long periods of time. They had to face the elements, harsh landscape, encounter many dangers, but to do so they could not be distracted by the frailties or limitations of the body. Many times when being chased, they had to cross landscapes that would kill most other people. These scouts had no provisions and equipment, relying solely on their ability to control the mind and body. Thus, to the scout, the harsh elements and dangerous landscapes were no obstacle. What was a living hell to all others was a home and sanctuary to the scout.

"This mastery of the body and mind was not all of thought, belief, and body control. Many times the scout had to face situations that would kill other men and by using only body control, the body would soon burn out. Even the scout's body would fail. What the scout used was a power greater than the control of body by the mind and belief. The scout would fuse his spirit to the elements and the land, thus becoming one. Once this fusion was complete, there was no separation, no pain, and no flesh. The struggle was transcended as the scout moved from the world of the force and into the world of spirit.

"So you see, there are times that it is not enough just to control the body and mind, for even that will not beat death. One must learn to fuse his spirit to that of land and the spirit world in order to rise above the limitations of the flesh."

With those words Grandfather left us to our own thoughts that night. We discussed what Grandfather had said, but we could not understand this spiritual fusion that he spoke of. We worked our way through the self-doubt as we went to sleep, desperately hoping that what we had learned about mind and body control would carry us through our journey. The night seemed to take forever. Sleep would have been great, but I was too excited about the journey we would begin the next morning. My mind also thought over Grandfather's words as I tried to understand all he said. I doubted very much if I got over an hour's worth of sleep, and I awoke in a state of mental exhaustion and physical fatigue. Not a very good way to start the long trek.

The morning broke bright and sunny, with hardly a cloud in the sky. The winds were raw and temperatures far below freezing. As agreed, we would not eat or drink anything through the whole trip, and the trip had begun when we awoke. We did not allow ourselves the luxury of a fire, for the fire would only make it more difficult to face the cold. Without a word to each other we left camp and headed south, leaving everything behind. Rick and I had wanted to duplicate the same kind of journey that a scout might face, so we kept up a fast pace, as if trying to escape some unseen enemy. What we did not realize was that the enemy we were really running from, and would ultimately have to face, was ourselves.

The first day was not very difficult, for we had often walked a full day in the cold without food, water, or rest. However, when the night finally overtook us, the landscape became difficult to negotiate in the dark and the travel slowed. Our energy began to drain. As we traveled into the night our pace slowed at times to half what it had been when we started out, and the lack of sleep exhausted us more. We dared not stop, for that was our unwritten pact, and much of the night was spent forcing our minds to push our bodies on. At times I began to hallucinate, seeing camp-fires that were not there or feeling that I was really asleep instead of walking.

The most difficult time of the first night came just before dawn. Though the winds had virtually stopped, temperatures had probably fallen deep into the teens. At times I could hardly bear the cold and began to shiver. It took a huge effort to bring my mind and body back under control again. I was draining my energy in the process and didn't realize it. Rick looked as though he was going through his own private hell, but neither of us could help the other. We barely spoke; talking would take effort, an effort we could not afford to waste. Any conversation would also be a dis-traction to the control of our mind and body, so we didn't risk it at all.

By sunrise we were in better spirits and our pace quick-ened again with the full sunlight. We pressed on through the morning so easily that it seemed to fly by without event. I felt as though I had gotten my second and third wind, but I did not know how. By mid-afternoon I began to grow fatigued again, more than I had been the night before. I began to worry about the oncoming night and whether I would make it or not. Self-doubt had hit me as hard as the fatigue. Still I pressed on, at times growing angry at myself and using that anger as a fuel for my drive; at other times I wanted to give up and cry. Even in the afternoon sun I could find no comfort or energy. I began to hallucinate more often, and the hallucinations became more real. I be-gan to stumble more frequently and fell hard a few times, barely able to get up and move my legs again.

By full dark I was beyond all my limits. I no longer walked but dragged my feet. Deep inside I felt that there was no way that we could ever finish the trip, for we hadn't even reached the halfway point. The cold and the lack of food, water, and sleep began to drain the last of our energy. Our minds could no longer control our bodies, and we both began to shiver violently. Walking became painful, with each step becoming a severe strain. We talked about giving up, but neither of us wanted to make that decision. As temperatures fell back into the teens the last of our energy drained. We had been defeated and we both knew it, and now we were too cold and drained to go on, or even to build camp. I thought that we would surely die.

My mind finally broke and my body collapsed. Rick came back to help, but he, too, collapsed. We lay there shivering, unable to move, and sick to our stomachs with exhaustion. I lifted my head to speak to Rick when I noticed that just up ahead a fire was burning. I thought that it was a hallucination but told Rick to look, anyway. Rick saw it too. Without a word we helped each other up and headed to the fire. Each step was painful, the shivering made our muscles hurt even more, but we stumbled on ahead. We both prayed that the fire was real, that someone was camping up ahead and we could get help.

We stumbled into a camp, half out of our minds with pain and fatigue. As we drew close to the fire Grandfather appeared from the darkness. I was so relieved that I began to cry uncontrollably as Rick, too, broke down and collapsed to the ground. I had to touch Grandfather to know that it was not a dream or a hallucination, and the fire warmed my soul. I was too tired to speak or react, and I could barely move. As the fire warmed me, Grandfather guided Rick and me into awaiting huts, and we collapsed into a profound sleep.

I was in and out of dream and reality for the next twenty-four hours. My body trembled with exhaustion and my mind swooned with fatigue. I dreamed that I was freezing to death and was too cold to get a fire started, only to awake in a cold sweat. I dreamed of endless walking with my legs twitching and muscles cramping in my sleep. At times I felt like I was being chased across a cold and barren landscape, with no place to hide and no natural materials for survival. Other times I just lay in a stupor of exhaustion; I could not discern between what was reality and what was dream. Most of all I dreamed about my death, feeling weak and frail, unable to confront the endless journey which still lived so vividly in my mind. Finally, as my body relaxed more fully, I was able to get periods of full and dreamless sleep, giving me much-needed reprieve from self.

I did not know how long I had slept. I could vaguely remember periods of light and dark, followed by another period of light and dark. I could not tell if my memory was real or a dream, but as I awoke, I felt stronger and my mind seemed clearer. As I crawled out of the hut I could feel my thighs burning in pain, and there were a few periods of dizziness I experienced and had to beat before I could stand. My walk was staggered and faltering as I approached the warm campfire. No one was around, so I sat down and went deep into a stupor of thought. I could not tell what day it was. Time and place had become a mystery; I wasn't sure if I had slept one night or two. I wasn't even sure where this camp was located, but I suspected that it was somewhere near the halfway mark on our trek.

With each passing sequence of thoughts and questions my mind grew clearer and my body became more stabilized. I began to feel so beaten and humiliated. The feeling of failure reached so deep that it affected every part of my thinking. It was as if this failure heralded the failure of my whole life. I had worked so long and hard and had so desperately wanted to succeed in this walk. To me it had become a rite of passage into the powerful life of a scout, but now it seemed that I was being denied entrance. The feelings of failure and humiliation reached deep inside, then turned to a raging anger. An anger directed toward myself. Anger at not achieving what I had wanted and anger because I had been so weak. I was so overwhelmed, so beaten, that I burst into tears. My mind was thinking in distorted ways and I had had enough. Rick suddenly appeared across from me at the fire, without uttering a word he sat down. I could plainly see that he, too, was crying.

We didn't look at each other, for each of us did not want to shame the other. To look at the other would only appear as a form of ridicule or would confirm the other's failure. So we kept our eyes close to the ground for a long time. Finally I spoke to Rick, trying to make him feel better, and also venting some of my self-doubt. We talked for hours about our ordeal. We discussed the journey, what we had felt, how we had controlled our bodies, and, most of all, how miserably we had failed. Talking helped us to realize that we were not alone in our failure but had both failed, and that took the sting out of the ordeal. During our conversation we both realized that Grandfather had been here, at this precise point waiting for us, and ultimately saved our lives. How could he have known where we would falter, and how could he get to this spot faster than we did? We had left him back at camp and traveled quickly, yet he still beat us there, made camp, a fire, and looked relaxed and free. We were baffled and perplexed as to how he could have accomplished this so easily, a journey that had nearly killed us both.

Grandfather's voice broke into our conversation with such power that both of us jumped. We had no idea where he had come from, but suddenly he was there, and our humiliation rushed back into our throats. As Grandfather spoke, there was no ridicule in his voice, nor did he say that we had failed. In fact, he was very kind and loving, and he told us that we hadn't failed at all. What we assumed to be a failure was just looked upon in the wrong way and distorted by our fatigued minds. Grandfather said, ''You did not fail just because you could not make it to your final goal. No one could have made that goal, at least not the way that you were going about the journey, not even the ancient scouts. In fact, I am surprised that you made it this far at all. You should be pleased.''

''But you once told us that the ancient scouts could easily make a journey like this. And you, yourself, beat us to the camp.''

Grandfather said, ''I said that no one could do that full journey the way you were doing it, not even I. Yes, the scouts could do that journey easily, but they would have used a far different technique than just control of body through mind, the fusion of self. For if anyone had attempted to do that journey the way you did the journey, they probably would have perished. What you both have done is to burn out your bodies and minds by draining your energy. When the energy wasn't replaced, then you began to falter and were beaten. But you were not beaten because of something you did wrong, for no physical energy can last forever. Your lack of knowledge as to how these things are done is what defeated you. Fusion of self is good for most things, but we reach a point where this is not enough, for the body and mind will burn out. What is needed is the fusion of spirit, which needs no energy or thought. That is what would have gotten you to your goal.''

''What is this spiritual fusion? How do we understand and use its power?'' Rick asked.

''You remember how I told you that most men live their lives as an island, as prisoners of the logical mind and the ego? I also taught that you must transcend this self to become whole. When you control the body through the belief of the mind, you begin to transcend the barrier of self. You begin to enter into the world of the force, the spirit-that-moves-in-all-things. You know that once this dimension is entered, you can touch that spirit, reach for instinct, all memory, and utilize the body and mind to their fullest. And you can utilize the primal mind and self. Even the life force helps when you are in this state of expanded self. But again, there is the limitation of physical self, and once those limits have been reached, there can be no more energy. This is what happened to you on the trek.''

''Then how could the scouts travel those incredible distances under severe conditions and through treacherous landscapes yet still survive easily? How could you beat us to this camp, have everything ready for us, and show no fatigue? Most of all, how did you know where and when we were going to collapse?'' I asked.

Grandfather answered, ''You will remember that I once said that all things were possible. If something was beyond human capability and our belief was strong enough, then all things could be done. If we could not do something on a physical level, then the spirit could carry us through. It is at this point, where the body is no longer capable of doing what we wish, that our absolute faith will carry us through and into the world of the spirit. It is in this world that we transcend all physical limitations and rise above all impossibilities. That is how the ancient scouts could flourish where most men would perish. That is how I was able to make this trip here so quickly, and that is how I knew exactly where you would have perished.''

''How can we use the spirit world?'' Rick and I asked almost simultaneously, excited now at the possibility.

Grandfather replied, ''I have already taught you how to enter the world of spirit. What I must do now is to show you how to work within that world and allow that world to work within you. The cycle of man's existence is the "I and ego" created prison. Then there is the world of the life force, which you already know. Beyond that world is the realm of spirit, and we must learn to use the power of the world. You go to the world of the life force, the primal mind, and all instinct by concentrating on that world, letting go all logical thought, and through belief. It was a conscious effort, a dynamic meditation, that brought you to the world of the sacred silence. This sacred silence became the vehicle that expanded your existence into the world of the spirit-that-moves-in-all-things.

"Now you must learn to enter the world of the spirit and to work within its power. It is a world that brings you closer to the sacred 'oneness.' For when a man becomes all circles and all cycles, he is then one with all things. It is not enough to get into these realms; you must know how to work within each power, so that you become the power and the power becomes you. What good is it to dwell in a world if that is all you can do? Getting to that world is just the beginning, the vehicle, but what you do there begins the cycle of power. This world of spirit is closer to the Creator; it is the world where all healing is found, where there is no time or place, a world where the body no longer exists and you transcend all flesh. Thus, living in this world would have made your winter trek a comfortable stroll, for you would have been walking in the spirit. When we walk in spirit, the body then falls away, and there are no limitations. The body is protected then, through the spirit, and the spirit has fused with the body.

"To get to this world of spirit you first must know where you are going. You then must believe that you can get there. It is the unwavering faith that becomes our doorway, and it is this faith that gives us power in the world of spirit. To enter the world of spirit you must have purpose, a purpose beyond the self. If the purpose is selfish, then the spirit realm is very difficult to enter."

I thought long and hard about what Grandfather was trying to teach. I could understand that to enter the spirit world there would have to be a direction. The direction, I knew, lay just outside the world of the life force. I could also understand that there must be pure faith, for nothing is done outside oneself without that faith. What I didn't understand was the purpose, a purpose without self. This, then, would not allow any exploration, practice, or learning of the spirit world, for that is for self.

"Couldn't we enter the spirit world if it was for the purpose of learning?" I asked.

Grandfather replied, "If you were to try to enter the spirit world for your own personal learning, then the spirit world should not be entered. But if you entered that world with the purpose of bringing back what you knew, to share that knowledge, then the purpose would be pure. The spirits will know if your motives and heart are pure. That is why great care should be taken to define the purpose before an attempt is made to enter that world. This way, when the purpose is clear and powerful, we can easily enter that world."

I asked, "Then how could I justify my purpose if it was only to make me walk in spirit to cover impossible distances and beat the cold? Am I not doing that just to see if I can duplicate what the ancient scouts had once done?"

Grandfather answered, "If that is your sole purpose, then you should not enter, but if it is something you can use to help another, then that world is yours."

Again I thought about this purpose. How could I be sure if a purpose was really pure and free of self, and how could I ever use it to teach someone? How could I make a difference in life by learning this? Was I just deluding myself? I could not see how using the spirit to walk that incredibly difficult journey could help anyone but me.

Grandfather broke into my thoughts, saying, "If you had to go and help someone that was many miles away, and you had to get to him using a journey such as this, would you make it there? Probably not, but if you did, you would be too exhausted to be of any help. Living in the spirit helps us transcend the limitations of our bodies so that the distraction of pain and exhaustion will not stand in our way. Ultimately, even in practice, you learn these things just to help someone. Your purpose then becomes pure and clear. Your purpose transcends self."

"But," I asked, "could we not use this to save ourselves in a dire survival situation, where we would otherwise die?"

"The purpose is still pure," Grandfather said, "because it protects the temple of the Creator. Remember always that you are the temple of the Creator, as is everyone and everything else. The Creator dwells in all things equally."

Grandfather continued with a certain warning in his voice. "A man who attempts to enter the spirit realm, the world of the unseen and eternal and then does not return to help others, has only selfish purpose. The spirit world will be denied to him. Thus, if you attempt to run to wilderness and hide from your responsibility of helping others, you will never fully understand the power of the spirit world."

"Then why have so many in the past gone into the wilderness to seek spirit and never returned to the worlds of man?" I asked.

Grandfather said, "Anyone can enter the world of spirit, especially in the purity of wilderness. The spirit world then speaks to each person individually, with more power being added to those who seek that world for the enlightenment of others. Thus if man's purpose is to selfishly run away and seek spiritual enlightenment for himself, then the spirit world will not give much of its power. But to those who seek that world purely and with a grander purpose, beyond self, then the power will be fully given to him.

"So," Grandfather went on, "what I am saying is that if a man enters the spirit world for only self, not only is the entry nearly impossible, but the wisdom added unto him will be of little value. That selfish man will never know the full rapture of the world of spirit, nor will he understand. He will never know how to work in that world or live in that world. He will view that world from afar, much like gazing into a fish tank. Yes, he will see that world, but he can never live within its power. He will always be alien, no matter how much he cloisters himself in the wilderness. The full power of the spirit world, then, is only for those working for a grander purpose and outside of themselves. Why should spiritual power be wasted on those who will not pass it down? It is only given fully and freely to those who work beyond the self. As each person needs the power it will be given to that person, exactly what is needed.

"So then, who needs more spiritual power? The man living in the purity of wilderness, where the living is easy and close to the Creator, or is it fully given to a pure man, trying to help his fellowman? The power, then, is only realized when one walks from wilderness and shares the power with all things."

"Then what good is living in wilderness if someone can be given more power living in the world of man?" Rick asked.

"It is in the purity of wilderness that we must learn, free from the distractions of man. It is wilderness that brings us close to the Creator and to the realities of life. Here in the bosom of creation all spiritual things are born, for creation is our temple, and it obeys the Great Spirit's every command. It is not a world built by the hands of man, influenced by the laws of society. Once the learning process in wilderness is over, however, a man must make frequent journeys into the world of man to share that which is taught by the purity of wilderness. All the great prophets and holy men have come from wilderness, for wilderness is where their spiritual fires were born. It is then, in wilderness, that man is given a choice. If he chooses to hide and seeks spiritual enlightenment only for himself, then his education is finished or limited at best. But for the one that leaves wilderness to give freely of the wisdom, there are no limits.''

Again there was a long period of silence as I thought about what Grandfather had said. It didn't seem fair to me that the power of the spirit world be given unequally. What Grandfather was saying was that if I chose to stay in the wilderness, then I would never fully know the powers of the spirit world no matter how badly I wanted that power. I would always be an outsider. But if I chose to bring this knowledge to the world, then there would be no limits to that power. I could not see why both could not live equally in the power of spirit, especially if they both were totally committed to spiritual enlightenment.

Grandfather's words broke into my thoughts. ''The power of the shaman, the power of the spirit world, is given only to those whose love is strong for his fellowman. To know the spirit-that-moves-in-all-things is to know that if one part of that spirit is sick, lost, or searching, then all is sick. To work only for the self is to know not the spirit-that-moves-in-all-things. If one does not know that spirit, one a does not know love and thus cannot transcend self.''

Though I did not like the thought of ever having to leave the wilderness, what Grandfather was saying made sense. If we were true to ourselves and lived within the spirit-that-moves-in-all-things, then we would know love. To love, then, is to work beyond the self, not for the spiritual enlightenment of self but for the enlightenment of all things. To stay in wilderness forever is to know no love, and selfishness will become a prison to the spirit. To love, one must truly be willing to sacrifice, for to heal the spirit of man, one heals himself. All of a sudden this seemed so simple, yet so complicated. We had talked about all the things to do when the spirit world is reached, but here I sat, struggling with the basic concepts of entering the spirit world. Everything was moving so fast, and I was so worried about leaving the wilderness that I totally lost sight of the fact that I had not even touched the world of spirit. At least not as Grandfather wanted us to do.

Grandfather's words again interrupted my thoughts, this time with a shock. He said, "To understand how to enter the spirit world and work within its power, you again must enter the water."

"Why the water again?" I asked. My voice cracked, shaking with fear.

Grandfather answered, "The water, the desert, the journey, mountains, chores, traffic, school, or society, they are all challenges, but the techniques to deal with them are all the same. I chose the water because you know the water and have faced cold water before."

"But I am burned out now and can barely stay warm as it is, even by the fire," I said.

"You will be exhausted and your energy depleted at so many times in life. It is at these times, when the physical limits are long passed and when we can go no farther, that we need to use the power of the spirit world. This is one of the many uses for that power, especially when you have no more strength. It is this power that makes all things possible."

Rick and I reluctantly followed Grandfather to the water near camp. As soon as we left the warmth of the campfire a deep chill came over me and I began to shiver. I had nothing left to ward off the cold. The journey had drained me to my limits. As we approached the water Rick and I stood there, still shivering and unable to move. I was paralyzed with the fear of having to enter the water. Even with my full reserve of energy it would have been difficult. My voice shivering, nearly out of control, I asked Grandfather if it wouldn't be better to wait until we had regained our strength. I told him there was no way I could enter the water, especially now, when I had nothing left inside me.

He replied, "Now is the best time, for that is when we especially need to transcend the body through the world of spirit."

"There is no way I can do this," I said. "I have no energy left to draw from and no amount of will or belief will keep me alive."

"It is now that you must go beyond giving in to the cold water. It can no longer be done with the belief of the mind or the control of the body. You have nothing left to energize your body and are at the limits of your mind. All the belief in the world cannot save you from those icy waters. In order to survive, you must slip into the world of spirit, and spirit will carry you through. The spirit knows no time or place, no body, and no thought. By living in the spirit there is no cold, no pain, no reality other than that of the spirit. Thus you become one with the spirit, and nothing in the physical world can harm you. You transcend the limitations of the body by becoming spirit, and your body is safe."

"But how do I enter this place of spirit?" I asked.

"You enter that world only through absolute belief, a purpose that is beyond self, and a purity of mind. It is the same as you have always done, as the still waters taught you on your second Vision Quest. Then you only looked at that spirit world but were not part of its power, nor did you know how to use its power. Now you must learn to live within the protection of that world and harness its power."

I replied, "I have belief; that is never the question. I have also learned to look at things through the pure mind, free of thoughts. But what purpose can I have for entering the waters? Is not entering the waters to see if I can be warm, for self-preservation, thus selfish?"

"If it teaches you, then, in your heart, will you use it to teach others?" Grandfather asked.

Without hesitation I said, "Yes!"

"Then that is purpose enough, as long as you know deep in your heart that you will use this to help someone else or to help the Earth."

I removed my clothes and walked to the water's edge, shivering more violently than ever. I had no idea what to do next, for Grandfather was not clear as to how to enter the world of spirit. All he said was that I already knew. I concentrated hard on my belief and purpose, making them the foremost part of my thoughts. Then I cleared my mind of all thought, closing my eyes to wash away the last remnants of analysis. Suddenly my mind seemed to surge and shift. My world shifted and I shifted worlds. It was at that moment that I found that I was no longer cold. I opened my eyes, and to my amazement I was neck-deep in the water. My body no longer seemed to exist, nor was the water like anything I had ever known. Time and place seemed no longer to exist, and my body and mind had no limitations. I walked from the water, dried by standing in cold winds, and put my clothes back on. Not because I had to but because I knew the lesson was over.

As I walked back to camp I could feel my logical mind beginning to slip back into the consciousness of reality. I grew cold again, but not to the point of shivering. It felt as though I had never entered the waters, because no new energy had been spent. I felt so alive and whole, for there had been no struggle in the water. Rick and I glanced at each other, smiling, for he, too, had entered the water.

We were both so full of rapture that there was no need for words, for each of us knew what the other was feeling. Instead we savored the silence of our souls. We had truly entered the world of spirit fully, and could use its power to go beyond our limitations. We had triumphed in the face of what we thought to be impossible. Grandfather had been right. All things are possible, if not in body and mind, then in spirit.

Grandfather had long since left camp without a word, leaving Rick and me alone. We lingered for a few more hours, then headed back to the Medicine Cabin. Though conditions were the same as when we had first started our journey, we walked faster and with no pain or fatigue. We hadn't eaten or slept very much, but the trek was no longer a trial. It held no power over us, for we walked in the spirit consciousness. Day or night, the journey seemed different than we had remembered. There was no sense of urgency, there was no cold, just a world full of the sense of spirit, a world full of joy. We understood now, for the first time, how the ancient scouts, and Grandfather, could make journeys such as this. Traveling in the consciousness of the spirit world was not only easier but put us into a greater reality that expanded the self. At that point I could not see why I would ever want to go through life any other way but in the world of spirit.

Grandfather had been waiting for us in the Medicine Cabin. Without hesitation he said, "Man cannot exist only in the world of spirit, for that, too, is selfish. There is work to be done in the world of physical reality, and to exist wholly in spirit is for the self. Man must then live a duality, part flesh and part spirit. He must walk between two worlds if he is to be effective. Until death releases us into the spirit world forever, we must live in both worlds. To live in the spirit world only becomes a form of death. We use the spirit world for guidance, for power to help us transcend self in times of limitations, and for helping others. The only danger comes when we live more in the world of spirit than in the world of physical reality. We must become a bridge between both worlds.

"You have learned to walk within the spirit consciousness even with the distraction of frigid waters. Live within this spirit world whenever there is an extreme need, when you have to face a reality that is beyond your physical and mental limitations. Use the spirit world for the clarity of your Vision Quest, to learn, and as a guide. As you have done in the waters, so can you do in the worlds of man. Go to the spirit world, then, anytime the distractions of man become a demon that threatens to tear you from your path. Go to that world when you must become a bridge for others, to help them along their path. When you walk within man's world, always be a bridge. For those who go there only for the glorification of self, the world of spirit remains out of reach and understanding."

5

Grandfather Explains Vision

I believe that the greater part of man's existence is in the spirit realm, the worlds of the unseen and eternal. It is the larger and purer part of life that makes life full and whole and makes man "one" with all things. This world is connected to all flesh, and all the entities of the Earth, sky, and water, and most of all to the world of the spirits. Ours is a universe of dynamic existence, where time and place do not exist and where man will never walk alone. The spirit world is rarely understood or seen by mankind today, for it has become a place that has long been abandoned for the gods of the flesh. Man has lost his connection to that world and thus his communication and power.

This world of spirit cannot be understood through the words and concepts of man, nor can it be understood by logical thought. It can only be entered through the heart and the pure mind. Thus modern man, caught in the mechanisms and rush of society, cannot imagine a world so vast and pure as the one I present. This world cannot be explained fully, for it must be lived. At best we can be given the tools that will allow us to communicate with and live within this world, but we cannot be led there on a physical level, especially not with the logical mind in tow. It is a world beyond our flesh, beyond our science and technology, and thus, to most, cannot exist.

In all of Grandfather's teachings he stressed the spiritual self most. In fact, living in the spirit and philosophy of Vision was stressed far more than any of the physical skills of survival, tracking, and awareness. These physical skills could not be complete without the spiritual knowledge that surrounded them. We lived in a world of society but spent most of our time in the wilderness with Grandfather. Our problem, even though we were young, was that society was teaching us one thing and the wilderness and Grandfather were teaching another. Despite this fact, there was no conflict, for we loved the philosophy of wilderness and spirit and in it found truth. The teachings of society never seemed real or viable, never worked in a pure environment like wilderness.

It was difficult for Grandfather to explain the workings of the spirit to us at times. I suspect that in the beginning we still clung to the attitudes and logic common to society. We had not yet learned to live through spiritual consciousness, so Grandfather made great efforts to teach us the wisdom and techniques of the spiritual mind. Once learned, we could explore the spiritual realities for ourselves, then build our own belief system. Grandfather gave us the tools we needed to live and communicate in the spirit world, but it was a long and slow process. One cannot lead another into a spiritual existence, only point the way.

We had begun to do Vision Quests a year before and had touched many of the spiritual teachings that Grandfather spoke of, yet we were still confused. We had attempted, and failed, to put the world of spirit into modern terms and language, and were frustrated because that type of thought process would always stand in the way of true spiritual enlightenment. We did not know how to meet the spirit world on its own terms and accept what was given with a spiritual mind. There was still a separation between ourselves and the spiritual realities of life. It wasn't until the end of my second Vision Quest that I first really touched and understood that world of spirit. It was then, in the height of my confusion and desperation, that Grandfather began to teach us how to live within, to understand, and to communicate with the spirit world.

It was the beginning of my second Vision Quest, and like the first, I was both frightened and excited with anticipation. It had only been a few months since my first quest, but its memory seemed distant and obscure. My first quest had not produced the spectacular results that I expected. Even so, I received insights into both my physical and spiritual life and began to understand many of the things Grandfather had taught me. I knew that something had changed deep inside me, for since that first quest I viewed life differently and felt closer to the Earth. I was disappointed, however, because I had not received anything similar to the magnificent Visions that I so often heard Grandfather tell of, though Grandfather had said that the most powerful Visions speak to us through nuance and imperceptible communication. He had said that my first Vision had been powerful, even though it had not met with my expectations. He had also said that it would teach me for the rest of my life.

I guess that most of the anxiety I felt about this second Vision Quest was due to my expectations. I expected and hoped that it would be better and more powerful than the first but at the same time anticipated that it would be nearly the same. I so desperately wanted a grand Vision, yet feared that I would only receive small insights such as I had been given during the first. Because of the lack of a grand Vision in my first quest, I felt that somehow it was the Creator's way of telling me that I was unworthy of a great Vision. Most of all I felt a block, an inability to communicate with the world of Earth and spirit, the way Grandfather so easily did. This lack of communication and my inability to communicate also caused me to feel unworthy, as if the spirit world might really have nothing to say to me.

With all of my doubts and expectations in tow, I left camp before first light and entered my Vision Quest circle full of fear and excitement. I had decided to take the quest in the same area as my first, feeling that there was more to be learned from that area. I felt secure there. Though the area was very confining and without a clear view, I still felt it was the best area for my second quest. Grandfather had always told us to select a quest area that afforded little view, for it would shut down our logical minds quickly through boredom. An area with a grand view would only give our minds something to feed on for days, thus slowing the Visionary process.

Grandfather was pleased with my preparations for this second quest and that I had chosen the same area, but he was not pleased with my attitude. He said, "You are entering the Vision Quest with too many expectations and ideas. It is best to go as an empty vessel, entering the quest as if you had no past, present or future. Thus you will be open to all things and will understand the communications you receive purely." He also said that I was too judgmental of myself and of my first Vision Quest. My attitude was obscuring the reality and power of my first Vision. Unless I shed the expectations and this disruptive attitude, it would affect and taint my second Vision Quest. Even with all his advice and warning, I still clung to all my expectations and prejudices.

The first day of the quest was a living hell. I could not settle down. My mind surged through all the self-doubt, expectation, and judgments. I began to remember vividly my first Vision Quest, as if it had just ended the day before. The isolation, loneliness, and all the boredom of that first quest seemed to fuse with this quest. As the two quests merged in my mind, the day became one long and endless nightmare. By the end of the first day I wanted to leave the area and go back to camp. I felt that I was just wasting my time and that the world of Vision had no place for me. When I finally fell asleep, it was profound, dreamless, and served as a much-needed break.

By the beginning of the second day my determination had grown strong again. I resolved that even if I got nothing from the quest, I was going to stay there until the end of the fourth and final day. In a way I was going to teach my body and mind a lesson of pain and boredom, feeling that my mind and body were somehow separated from my true self. At this point I could plainly feel a duality of self, like there was some greater part of me hidden and smothered by someone or something. In a way it felt like I was two people, yet at the same time one. It also felt as though I had two minds. The active mind, which I did not like, and an obscure but expansive mind, which was the one that wanted desperately to emerge.

By the middle of the second day my resolve to stay had eroded and I was filled with self-doubt again. I over-analyzed everything, every nuance of nature, every movement, and every thought, but there was nothing real. Nothing communicated with me. Nature felt like it had turned its back, and I even felt that my prayers ended somewhere in my throat. Again I had the sickening feeling that I was not worthy, that the Vision Quest was for other, more powerful and righteous people but not for me. I even began to think that it was because I was not of Native American blood, but Grandfather had said that the Vision spoke to all people, no matter what they were or believed. He said, "The spirit world is there for everyone but only touched by those who believe purely."

"Believe purely." Those words resounded in my head on the morning of the third day as I awoke. Somehow I had given in to sleep, and the night passed unnoticed. Certainly I believed in the world of spirit. I had seen it so often manifest in the life of Grandfather and in the purity of wilderness. I had borne witness to miracles and had seen their power. Of course I believed, and believed without a doubt. I thought to myself then that the problem must be in the word, purely. Somehow I was not pure, or I wasn't looking at the spirit world in the right way, in a pure way. I did not know how to find this purity about which Grandfather spoke.

All day long I thought about the purity of mind and what that meant. The search for answers filled my day and saturated my every thought. I concentrated so hard on finding answers that I forgot I was questing, and unconsciously I left the area and began to wander, deep in thought. I must have wandered for hours, finally ending up sitting on the bank of the stream near the camp area but still unconscious of the fact that I was supposed to be in my quest area. It was as if another part of myself had taken me to the stream.

I looked into the water for a long time, watching the whirlpools, ripples, and quiet areas. I noticed the perfect reflection of the landscape in the quiet water, and there, along with the reflection of everything else, was a reflection of me. It was so clear that I might just as well have been looking into a mirror. Then suddenly the wind surged and stirred up the surface of the water, the reflection jarred, split into thousands of images, and was gone. All that was left was the turbulence of the water's surface and all else had vanished. As I looked at the imageless surface, the word *thought* thundered into my head, and suddenly I knew what Grandfather had meant by *purity*. It was then that I realized that I was not in the quest area.

I rushed back to the quest area, fearing that I had broken some ancient rule and that surely the Creator would punish me for leaving the area. At the same time I was overjoyed at the tremendous insight I had gained at the water's edge. I was so overjoyed that I could barely stop laughing as I ran back to the quest area. I had gotten an answer, a big answer, and now I could at least use the rest of the quest time to try to fully understand its power. As far as I was concerned, I got more than I had bargained for. The answer to the question of purity was a greater gift than even a grand Vision. I was absolutely thrilled and overjoyed.

Finally returning to the quest area and settling back in, I began to think about the waters. I had heard Grandfather refer to the "purity of the reflection in quiet waters," but I had never fully understood it until now. The mind was like the water. When there was no thought, no analysis, no movement, and only purity, there was a perfect reflection of Nature. When there was thought, the water would move and there could be no reflection. I still felt a need for more answers because I knew that there must be a connection to the world of spirit. The world of Nature had been perfectly reflected in those still waters, and somehow the world of spirit must do the same. But I could not figure out how.

As the sun set on the third day I realized that part of my problem had been my expectations, self-doubt, over-analysis, and judgment, just as Grandfather had said. My mind cleared as I gazed into the sky, and I felt as though

I were seeing the first sunset of my life. As I looked about the Pine Barrens, now free of thought and expectation, everything looked fresh, real, and very different. The world was new and wondrous, free and pure. Yet every time a word of description would enter my mind, the world would change and go back to the way I always remembered. It was a duality in perception, feeling, and thought. Two worlds and two separate realities, similar but very different.

On the fourth and final day I felt a sense that I was running out of time. Time hardly existed and the day was so full of new experiences that it just slipped away. There was so much I wanted to do and experience with my new way of looking at the world. I was afraid that I would lose what I had learned when I left the quest area and returned to camp. Or worse yet, to the world of man. I could feel the fear well up within me as the night approached, and I knew that I was close to ending the quest. Determined to keep this feeling for as long as possible before it vanished when I had to walk out, I stayed awake all night. I just didn't want the last day of ecstasy to end.

Well into the night, past the point of utter exhaustion, I explored this beautiful new world. At times I allowed my mind to be active in what I called "my old mind." I thought that it was just enough to savor this new gift for just a day, for I had gained so much. Even if I lost its power back in the world of man, I would always remember this purity as one of the greatest gifts. As I gazed out onto the final sunrise of the quest, in purity of thought and in the rapture of Nature, I felt something moving, something strange and beautiful. Deep in the pure reflection of my mind I knew that it was spirit. It was then that I understood that this pure world that I had been living in for the last days of the quest was also the world of spirit.

Slowly and reluctantly I walked back to camp, deep in

thought about the past few days. As I went, I could feel
the spirit consciousness of the pure mind begin to slip from
me, and as my head began to refill with all manner of
thoughts, it was gone. I tried to get it back, but my thoughts
would not yield any ground. I sadly walked to the stream,
where I had been the day before, and gazed back into the
waters. There were no still images, for the wind was
blowing, and I felt so overwhelmed by my loss that I began
to cry. The wind ceased for a moment, and I looked back
toward the water, my eyes still filled with tears. There on
the surface was reflected the perfect picture of Nature and
of me.

As I gazed at the water, off in the corner, I was startled
to see the reflection of Grandfather, also gazing at the water. Before I could turn and speak a word, he said, "End
your sorrow, for you have lost nothing. Just because you
have ended the quest does not mean that you have to lose
what you have gained. For that is one of the many reasons
that we quest, to gain insight and wisdom that we can use
in all worlds." With that he turned and walked away. I
looked up and behind me, but he had vanished down the
trail. As I looked back to the stream and out into the cedar
swamp, the purity of mind and the rapture of the spirit mind
filled me, and I was again back in the spirit consciousness.
I was filled with rapture as I wandered back to camp.

Periodically along the way I stopped my thoughts to see
if I could still view Nature through the spiritual mind. I felt
like a small child, peeking around a corner to see if the
presents were still under the Christmas tree. Though at
times it was difficult to shut down the whirl of thoughts
going on in my mind, I could still reach a point of purity.
Each time I did, the landscape, my feelings, and my perceptions changed, and I would be transported into that purity of reflection. I vowed that I would always keep

practicing this new purity so that I would never lose its power. For the first time I could really see.

Grandfather sat at camp as if awaiting my return. As soon as I entered camp, he motioned me to sit down, giving me no chance to put away my things or to speak. He looked at me for a long time with a half smile on his face that said he knew exactly what had taken place. It was a smile that also said, "See, I told you." Finally he spoke. "You were not wrong to leave the quest area on the third day, because your heart guided you to the water. Not only were you given the wisdom of the purity of mind from the water, but the water also communicated with you. The water spoke to you, not in the tongues of man but in the language of the heart, and you heard its words. This has been a powerful Vision, a grand Vision, a Vision of spiritual understanding and communion."

We did not discuss my quest any further that day, as was custom. Grandfather knew all he needed to know, and now I had to give him time to himself before he would talk more. I also needed the time to rest, to play, and to think. I hadn't realized at the time that I had a spiritual communication with the waters. I had been too amazed at what they had taught me and had not taken the time to think about how that wisdom had come to me. I had gone to the water unconsciously, drawn there by another mind, and at the water I found an answer. I knew now that some spirit, possibly the spirit of the water, had drawn me to it to drink of its wisdom. I knew that it wasn't coincidence, for there was so much power and wisdom, and it was directed right at my heart.

I don't think that I can remember a day before this one where I felt more alive or where Nature was more real and intense. I was in a world so different than I had ever known. It was a world full of beauty, rapture, and a sense of expansion. A pure world, untainted by the things of man, my analysis, or my thoughts. All through the day I could sense so much more. My awareness seemed to have peaked to a level of that beyond the physical senses, and I could sense things moving far outside my realm of perception. The dimensions of my self had dissolved and fused with that of the world around me, and I could feel no limitations to that self.

As night drew closer, the sense of knowing that there was more moving out there in Nature than just the physical world overwhelmed my mind. I could feel a spiritual sense to all that was. It was a world so different than the one I knew before, and I could have it anytime I wanted. The real test, I thought, would come when I had to go back to the world of man. That thought bothered me the most, because it was a world away from Nature, removed from the purity of spirit and separated from the laws of the Creator. Though I feared going back, I was excited in a way, for I wanted to see if I could hold on to this power in the world outside the wilderness. That, I thought, would be the real challenge and the test that would determine whether this new wisdom had really become part of me.

As the night grew late I fell into a state that was somewhere between exhaustion and introspection. Grandfather began to speak about the quest and communication with the world of spirit. At the time there was a lot that I could understand immediately. But there was much that I did not. With a coyote teacher this was always the way. He always went beyond the lesson at hand, with information that was meant to take us farther than what we had just learned, information that would open the way for more teaching that we could use in the future, wisdom we would have to think about for a long time before we could ever understand, teachings that I still remember to this day.

He said, "Man is like an island, a circle within circles. Man is separated from these outer circles by his mind, his beliefs, and the limitations put upon him by a life away from the Earth. The circle of man, that island of self, is the place of logic, the 'I,' the ego, and the physical self. That is the island that man has chosen to live within today, and in doing so he has created a prison for himself. The walls of his island prison are thick, made up of doubt, logic, and lack of belief. His isolation from the greater circles of self is suffocating and prevents him from seeing life clearly and purely. It is a world of ignorance where the flesh is the only reality, the only god.

"Beyond man's island of ego, his prison, lies the world of the spirit-that-moves-in-all-things. It is a world that communicates to all entities of creation and touches the Creator. It is a circle of life that houses all of man's instinct, his deepest memory, his power to control his body and mind, and bridges the world of flesh. It is a world that expands man's universe and helps him to fuse himself to the Earth. Most of all, it is a world that brings man to his higher self and to spiritual rapture.

"There is a circle beyond the circle of the force: the world of spirit. Man is also in this world, for his spirit walks also in this land of the spirit. Here man finds a duality in self, where at one moment he walks in flesh and then again in spirit. It is a world of the unseen and eternal, where life and death, time and place, are myths. A place where all things are possible. A place where man transcends self and fuses with all things of Earth and spirit. It is a place closest to the Creator and to the limitless powers of creation. Beyond this place is the consciousness of all things, the final circle of power before the Creator.

"Man living in the island of self is living but a small part of what life is all about. Man must transcend the barriers, the prisons of ego and thought, and reach the Creator. All islands, all circles, must be bridged. Each world must be understood, then finally fused into an absolute and pure 'oneness.' Then there can be no inner or outer dimension, no separation of self, just a pure oneness where man is at once all things. It is in this fusion of worlds that man will know all things and live the deeper meanings of life. Man then moves within all things, and all things move within man. Then and only then can man ever hope to touch God.

"Modern man cannot know the worlds, these circles, beyond his own ego. The logical mind will never allow man to expand beyond the ego or the flesh, for that is where the logical mind feels safe. Modern thought is the prison of the soul and stands between man and his spiritual mind. The logical mind cannot know absolute faith, nor can it know pure thought, for logic feeds upon logic and does not accept things that cannot be known and proved by the flesh. Thus man has created a prison for himself and his spirit, because he lacks belief and purity of thought. Faith needs no proof, nor logic, yet man needs proof before he can have faith. Man then has created a cycle that cannot be broken, for if proof is needed, there can be no faith.

"You have had no problem with belief, for you have witnessed many things that cannot be explained in modern terms, yet you know them to exist," Grandfather said, expecting no response. "Your problem with your first Vision Quest and part of the one you just had was that your mind would not shut down. Your mind would not let you see with spiritual consciousness. That is the problem with man today, for he cannot purify his mind. You learned from the purity of still water, and you saw creation for the first time in a pure way. When you opened your mind to that purity, you also opened a path to your greater self, beyond the island of the ego. You learned to listen and to see through your heart and not your logical, overbearing mind.

"The world of inner Vision and spirit does not communicate to us in words or logic, as you have found. Instead that world communicates to us through dreams, Visions, symbols, signs, and feelings. Most of all the communications are subtle, many times escaping our perceptions, for they can only be felt when the mind is pure and without thought. When our mind is filled with thought, there can be no room for spiritual things, and we take no notice of subtle communication. That is why we must quiet ourselves frequently or walk within the pure mind; otherwise we miss so much.

"When you go to the world of man," Grandfather warned, "you must go to the pure mind often, for the distractions of man are many. You must open yourself to the world beyond flesh so that you continue to walk close to the Earth, or the complacency of society will consume you. Your mind will become like theirs. When you walk within the world of man, it is more difficult to find the quiet of the pure mind, for the consciousness of man seeps into every part of your being. But by going to that pure mind, not only do you know reality but also you pull all those around you into that purity. Thus you affect the spirit-that-moves-in-all-things in a positive way. You become a light in the darkness of flesh and logic. You become a bridge to the outer worlds.

"But take care," he continued, "for the power of the modern world will infect your thinking. You must take care to know the difference between real spiritual communication and consciousness and that consciousness born of the fantasies of logical mind. This can only be done by removing yourself from the rush of society and by finding that purity without the demons of distraction. It is the distractions of man and his thinking that can distort the spiritual mind and give us half-truths and feelings. You must learn to function within the realms of man, for that will be your greatest test. The pure mind, the spiritual consciousness, will keep you close to the philosophy of oneness, even when all around you is in chaos.''

Dawn was beginning to show on the distant horizon when Grandfather finished speaking. My head swooned with all that had been said. There was so much I didn't yet understand, and much that frightened me. The things that I did understand helped me put together a clearer picture of the spirit world and the way it communicated to us. It helped me answer so many questions, though it raised so many others. I fell asleep right where I sat, a sleep that was so deep and profound that it carried me into the following morning. I awoke to the horrible thought that not only had I wasted a day sleeping but that I had to go back to society for a few days.

As I walked home I could hear the distant noises of civilization drawing closer. It was like facing an ominous demon that would soon feed upon my soul. With each step closer to the outside world I felt more alone and confused. Going into spiritual mind became more and more difficult as I drew closer to the pavement, noise, and commotion that lay just outside the Pine Barrens. I passed a pile of garbage that lay alongside one of the trails and knew that I was back in man's world. Though my home was on the edge of the Pine Barrens, the rich aroma of pine gave way to the stench of fumes and garbage. The sweet song of birds and winds in the oaks gave way to the roar of man's reality. I felt lost.

For the next four days I went through a living hell. It was still summer and I didn't have to face school, but being so close to civilization was almost impossible to bear. I know that my father could sympathize with me, for I often

heard him speak of his excursions into the Scottish coun-
tryside and how he hated coming home. Unlike me, he had
to return to the city of Glasgow, which really must have
been a shock to the system. At least I could talk to him
about the way I felt, and someone outside of the sanctuary
of the pines would understand. That seemed to help, but I
still longed for the purity and freedom of wilderness.

For the first two days back in civilization I could not get
back to the purity of mind that I had experienced in the
woods. Even when I thought I was getting close to that
purity, something always felt tainted and unpure. It seemed
to be that my mind would not let go, or that somehow it
was being affected by outside thoughts. It was only out of
desperation on the third day that I went out from the yard
and back into the woods for a few hundred yards that I was
even able to come close to that purity. It seemed that the
closer to civilization I was, the harder it was to get into
that spiritual consciousness. At least the last few days in
civilization were not as bad as the first, for I could get close
to that purity. I just had to get away from things for a while
to get close.

Finally all the chores were done and I had another few
days of freedom, so back to the woods I went. It felt as
though I were going home, and I nearly ran the entire way.
I really wanted to talk to Grandfather about my inability to
get back what I had learned in the Vision Quest. School
would start in a few weeks and I desperately needed to
know how to rise above the strangling consciousness and
distraction of society. I could not imagine going back to
school and being imprisoned for nearly half a day, every
day. Well, I could at least look forward to the islands of
freedom called weekends.

Grandfather gave me a broad smile when I ran into camp,
carrying the stench of civilization with me. He looked quiet

and serene, as if he had spent the whole week with God. In a way it made me angry to think that I had to go back to civilization at all. Grandfather always seemed to embody the power of wilderness and spirit no matter where he was, even when he went into civilization. Though this was rare and he only seemed to be passing through, I suddenly realized that whenever he went through man's world he remained unaffected, as if he carried the wilderness with him. I came right out and asked him how he managed to keep moving within the spirit even when moving within man's world. I hadn't realized it was the first thing I'd said to him.

He smiled and said, "I'm fine, how are you?" I said that I was sorry for not saying hello first and sat down near the fire, deep in thought. He said, "I knew exactly what would be on your mind when you returned, even before you left camp. You ask one of the grandest questions of all times. You want to know how to live within the confines of man's world yet still exist in the purity of spirit." He continued, not awaiting my confirmation. "Grandson, if I could give you an easy answer, I would. There is no easy answer, no one answer, for each man must find the way himself. It is a very long and difficult path and a constant struggle. That is why so many spiritual people will not leave the security and purity of the wilderness, for to stay in wilderness only, the path is very easy. As you have seen."

"Then why do I have to go back?" I asked in a frustrated and angry tone.

"Because," he replied, "that is what you have to do now, and where your Vision will lead later. You have learned much about life and reality this past season. You should know that your school will not make a prison or steal your freedom. For freedom is in your mind, and so is the prison. It is your choice, just as you choose to carry the spirit with you or choose to allow the spirit to be taken from you by the worlds of man. Everything in life is a choice. It is a choice to follow spirit or flesh, and it is your choice that determines where you must live. No one is responsible for you but you.''

I was struck into immobility by his words. I had never looked at things like that before. I never looked at life as being a choice before, far less the things of spirit. Suddenly a huge burden was lifted from me, yet I did not know why. Something had shifted and changed inside of me, though it was nothing tangible. All I knew was that school did not look so bleak, nor did society, for I had a choice. I had always had a choice but never realized it until now. I will always have a choice. A choice to seek flesh or spirit and a choice to run from my Vision or to live it fully. The waters had taught me another great lesson. I had a choice to have a clear and still surface or to live in turbulence. The lessons of the waters never seem to end.

6

Jesus

There was very little that Grandfather could say or do that would shock me. His life was full of miracles. Each day I learned something new and startling about Nature, survival, tracking, and awareness. Each day, too, without fail, I learned something new about the world of spirit and man's spiritual existence. The things of the spirit are what Grandfather stressed most, and these spiritual attitudes and techniques were taught far more than anything else. It was not a world of talk or of useless concepts that only worked for a select few. The world of spirit and spiritual power could be had by all at any age. The things that he taught were so simple and pure that we could go right out and achieve them. Though these things were simple, they were very profound and powerful. Thus, walking in the spirit world and bearing witness to miracles became part of our everyday lives. After a while we just accepted these things. Things that most people would hold in awe, we took for granted.

After living with Grandfather and his teaching for a few years I thought I had an idea of most of the things he knew of. That was until he began to talk about Jesus. Granted, Grandfather was a man who had wandered for nearly sixty-three years of his life and had been many places and learned many things. But when he began to quote passages of the Bible, I was so shocked that I couldn't speak, so I just listened. I thought I knew quite a bit about the Bible, for I went to church most Sundays with my parents. A good part of my upbringing revolved around Bible teachings, at least at home. Hearing the Bible and the life of Christ interpreted by Grandfather in such a simple, pure, and profound way made sense for the first time. Though he talked of Christ many times, the first time was the most complete and powerful, and I will never forget even the smallest detail. The event changed my life and the perceptions I had about the Bible and Jesus.

Grandfather, Rick, and I had been hiking all day and had rarely taken the time for a break. We wanted to get to one of our southern camp areas near Prophecy Hill before dark so that we could spend the entire next day learning and exploring. It was late spring, but we were still in school, so every moment of our weekends was precious. I had just turned thirteen that winter, and in the eyes of Grandfather I was a man, though still very much a student. As we walked, my mind was filled with the many things I had learned over the past years. I had learned the fusion of self and spirit, learned to dwell within the power of the spirit world, and seen the power and teachings of the Vision Quest. I was also beginning to touch the wisdom of true invisibility and the dimension of the veil that knew no time or place yet held all history. I had seen Grandfather heal the sick when all modern medicine had failed, and my life was so full of mysteries yet to be learned that my mind seemed like it could handle no more.

I thought, too, how different my world and beliefs were from my parents, my acquaintances, and from society.

We were passing along the trail near the entrance to Prophecy Hill when Grandfather abruptly stopped and left the trail. He was headed straight to the old graveyard, as if urgently called by some unknown spirit. We followed but could barely keep up with him, such was his determination to get to wherever he was going. Once in the graveyard, he walked straight to the south end, an area that we had not yet explored. Pushing through some briars we entered a small clearing, full of new green grasses, brilliant sunshine, and several gravestones. At the far end of the clearing a stone cross had nearly fallen over with age. Grandfather went to the cross and, with a determination I had never seen before, straightened the cross. Without hesitation, we also helped. Grandfather put some rocks around the stone cross to keep it upright, offered a prayer, then sat down in silence. Rick and I were absolutely confused as to why he had taken the time and gone so far out of his way to fix a fallen cross.

Grandfather sat for a long time gazing at the cross, then he finally spoke the words that still resound in my mind and life. He said, ''I am in awe of this man called Jesus. He was a man of purity, of wilderness, a prophet and a teacher, a man who walked close to the spirit. He healed the sick, raised the dead, and fed the masses. His life was so full of truth, and he lived that truth. His life is the example of what we all should strive to become. This Jesus was so full of love for his people that he gave up his life for them. Yet death had no power over him, and he was taken home to the Creator. The evil ones could kill his flesh but not his spirit. Thus this man has inspired more nations and healed more people than I could ever dream of. Yet what we do to his name and teachings today has distorted that truth.

"Jesus was such a simple man. He had no real home, for like the place of his birth, he preferred the wild places. His temples were the gardens, the mountains, the shore of the sea, and the wilderness. To him, whenever two or three were gathered with him, then that was his church, his temple. His clothing was simple, he carried no supplies, and he let the Creator and Nature take care of his every need. His teachings were simple, yet they were profound truth. To him there were no customs, traditions, or ceremonies to imprison him. Nor did he pass down in his teachings much in the way of ceremony. Instead, what he taught and worshiped was a simple purity. Why today have his teachings become so complicated? Why are there so many ceremonies and customs surrounding his name, when all he taught was simplicity?

"The distortion of truth lies in man's quest to complicate all that is simple and pure. Doctrine and ceremony are argued, churches and temples are separated, and man strives to complicate more. What should be, is a striving to bring back the simple truths, unadulterated by man's ceremonious crutches.

"What man seems to have done is to pick the Bible apart to make each part to fit his own personal needs and religion. By taking the Bible apart, man has removed each part from the context of the whole and has lost the true meaning of things. I have even heard that modern man has argued the translation of the Bible and has argued over the meaning of one single word. The single word, or the single passage, is now what is important. What is really important is the overall meaning and the basic truth. Man must stand back from the Bible and read it as a whole. For only when man soars like the wingeds and looks down upon the Earth from the lofty heights will he understand his place upon the Earth. Man must do the same with the Bible, or, for that matter, all religion and religious works.''

Grandfather paused for a long moment, probably to collect his thoughts and to give us time to think. He spoke with a passion and a conviction, at times almost appearing angry at what man had done to the teachings of Christ. There was a profound truth in what he was saying, for so many times I had witnessed the same thing happening to those teachings. I had seen people pick apart the Bible and use one verse or passage to fit their needs. Yet by removing that passage or verse from the whole, they distorted the meaning and twisted the teaching. I had seen a verse used to illustrate a point, then several weeks later the same verse was used to illustrate the opposite truth. This way, by taking a verse from the context of the entire teaching, man has enabled himself to use the teaching as a weapon against those who oppose his beliefs. It seemed to me that most disagreements came from the interpetation of the verse rather than from the entire context of the truth in the writings. So then the separation in the churches and temples of man lay in these interpretations of the verse or passage. The overall truth should not be misinterpeted or distorted.

I finally rallied enough courage to ask Grandfather a question, still stunned by what he had said. ''What, then, are the simple teachings of the Bible and Jesus?'' I asked.

He hesitated for a moment, then answered the most pressing question on my mind, the question I had been afraid to ask. He said, ''You wonder how the teachings of the Bible and of Christ are in conflict or are similar to what I have been teaching you. In the past, all you have seen is the conflict and not the truth. What I teach, what Nature teaches, is the same basic truth the Bible teaches. The only distortion and conflict is caused by man and his interpeta-

tion of what I teach, compared to the teachings of the Bible.
When you look from afar, there are more things similar
than are different. There is no conflict in your mind and in
the minds of man. For what man has done to the Bible and
the teachings of Jesus he has done with so many other
religions and philosophies. In essence there is a common
thread that binds all religions and beliefs together. From
that thread of truth man has complicated his world with
doctrine and ceremony, and man becomes detached from
that truth. His interpetations stand in the way of that truth
and obscure the similarities in all beliefs. Then there is
conflict, not in the truth but in the doctrines.

"You will remember that I told you that faith and belief
are the most powerful forces on Earth and of the spirit.
Jesus taught the same thing, only in a slightly different way.
Jesus said, 'I tell you the truth. If anyone says to this mountain, "Go, throw yourself into the sea," and does not doubt
in his heart but believes that what he says will happen, it
will be done for him. Therefore I tell you, whatever you
ask for in prayer, believe that you have received it and it
will be yours.' Jesus also said, 'Everything is possible for
him who believes.' As I have told you, and as Jesus taught,
belief is the most powerful force on Earth and of the spirit.
For through belief all things are possible. You will remember that belief was important before you fused body and
mind as one. It was also important when you fused the
world of flesh to the world of spirit, and this absolute belief
is the basic truth of all healing. This belief empowers all
things."

Grandfather continued explaining the similarities to what
he taught and the teachings of the Bible. "You will also
remember that I taught you that love is what drives us from
the wilderness to help the lost and searching masses. Love
causes us to give up many of our dreams, for that love is

more powerful than our dreams. To know the spirit-that-moves-in-all-things is to love. Love, too, is a great power, for it motivates us to empower others. Jesus also said, 'Love your enemies.' Christ taught us to lay down our lives for others. Laying down one's life does not always mean death but giving up some of the things that we cherish in order to love and help others. To be willing to sacrifice all for your brothers and sisters is to know the power of love.

"So, too, have I told you that the wilderness is truth and that the prophets came from the wilderness. John the Baptist came from the wilderness, for it was in the purity of wilderness that the Creator spoke to him. John said, 'I am the voice of one calling in the desert.' Jesus also used the wilderness as a teacher. The Bible says, 'At once the Spirit sent him out into the desert, and he was in the desert for forty days, being tempted by Satan. He was with the wild animals, and the angels attended him.' Was this not a Vision Quest? Jesus fasted for those forty days and it was there that he was tested by evil. Is it not the same Vision Quest that guides and teaches you, as I have taught you? So does not the Bible teach the purity of wilderness and the power of the Vision Quest?"

There was again a long pause in our conversation, and my mind came rushing back in to try to digest all that Grandfather had said. I had remembered so many stories of John the Baptist. The wilderness was where he wandered, where he learned, and where John had touched God. John came from wilderness, just as Christ went to the desert wilderness. So, too, did all the great prophets. For the first time I could see the similarity in what he did to our own Vision Quest. I felt the power and purity of the wilderness in the Bible and in the teachings of Jesus. To Christ the wilderness, the gardens, and the mountains were also his temples, for that is where he taught. I felt drawn to go back and reread the Bible, this time with simple purity and to study it as a whole. What amazed me more still was Grandfather's ability to quote verses from the Bible. I had no idea until then that he knew anything of the Bible or of Jesus, yet what he told us revealed a tremendous amount of thought and study.

Grandfather began to speak of prayer and how it was similar to our meditation, which he called the "sacred silence." He said, "Jesus taught people that it would be best to pray in a closet. Most people interpret this as a way of not proclaiming one's spirituality publicly, but I suspect that there is much more to that teaching. A basic truth that escapes most men. Jesus said, 'But when you pray, do not be like the hypocrites, for they love to pray standing in the synagogues and on the street corners to be seen by men. When you pray, go into your room, close the door, and pray to your Father, who is unseen.' By going into the silence of your room and closing the door, you seclude yourself. The distractions of man fade away and there is but you and the Creator. As I taught you to pray in the Sweat Lodge for these same reasons, Jesus also taught, but in a different way.

"There is much teaching in the Bible that is difficult even to attempt to discuss fully. Each teaching must be looked at wholly, for even I as I talk to you, I have taken many things out of context. What you must learn to do, with any teaching, is to look beneath the most apparent meaning for other deeper meanings. Then compare that meaning to the whole to understand what is true. But the final test of that truth is to take it to the purity of wilderness and see if it works there. For in the wilderness is the temple of creation.

"Take these things also into the depths of your heart, for there you carry all things. If it is true to your heart, then it is true to all things and all people. Finally, look for the common truth in all religions and philosophies. Seek out the simplicity and throw away all that is complicated, for it obscures the truth. I cannot judge any religion, philosophy, or doctrine, for if it is true to the believer and works for all men, then it is truth. My purpose, then, is not to judge but to find the simple truth.

"So, too, have I taught you," Grandfather continued, "that creation will provide for you. I have shown to you that possessions are not important, just the things of the spirit. Jesus then taught the same things when he told his people not to be concerned with what they will eat, or how they will clothe themselves. He said that the Creator will provide all of these things for us. Jesus also said, 'Do not store up for yourself treasures of Earth, where moth and rust destroy and thieves break in and steal.' Jesus went on to teach that the most important things in life were not of the flesh. We should not concern ourselves with the things of the flesh, for the true riches in life can only be found in our hearts and spirits. The things that all men work for are peace, love, joy, and purpose, and these things will never be found in the false gods of the flesh. For they can only be found in our hearts and in the things of the spirit.

"The Bible also teaches what I teach about healing. I have told you that the healer is but a bridge. The healing takes place only through the power of the Creator. I have shown you that you must never take credit for these things, for the ego will destroy the healing. Jesus, after healing the man with leprosy and again when he healed the blind and dumb, said, 'See that no one knows of this.' Christ taught his people that it was of no purpose to take credit for anything. That we should work our power in a quiet way, so that no man should marvel. This also teaches that we should not allow our egos to interfere with those things of the spirit, for the ego obscures the truth.''

I was taken aback by Grandfather's reference to healing in the Bible. I could not see why Grandfather would say that was similar to what he taught, for most men believed that only Jesus could heal. It was not a gift for mortal man. I asked, ''Does it say in the Bible that we are to have the power to heal, or is that just meant for Jesus?''

Grandfather replied, ''Jesus himself commanded his people to heal. Jesus commanded, 'Heal the sick, raise the dead, cleanse those who have leprosy, drive out demons. Freely you have received, freely give.'

''You see, Jesus did not ask, but commanded us to heal. The age of miracles is not over, for that same command still lives in all of us. It is a basic truth for all people, for even you have borne witness to so many healings and so many miracles.''

Grandfather stood, looked up toward the righted cross, back to us, then said, ''You both wonder why I went out of my way to right this cross. That question I cannot fully answer, for there are many reasons, but they can only be understood by the heart. The important thing is that the cross is a symbol of the teachings and prophecies of Jesus, and it is further a symbol of someone's religion, whether we perceive it in our minds as good or bad, right or wrong, or whether we see the similarities or not. To truly love is also to respect another's beliefs and afford him the right to worship as he chooses. Each religion and belief has something to teach us, if we are pure and open enough to listen. All things have the common thread, which is truth.'' With those words Grandfather walked back to the trail and we headed south.

We finally got to the camp area, much later than we had anticipated. It was more than worth being late, for we had learned so much. We never bothered to build shelters but satisfied ourselves with a fire. The night was warm, and we would be more than content to lie on the ground and sleep near the fire. There was little conversation around the camp-fire, at least none concerning what Grandfather had said about the teachings of Jesus. I was so eager for more, but there was already so much to digest and try to understand. I was amazed at how much clearer the teachings of the Bible were now that Grandfather had clarified them. Up until this time I thought I knew more about the Bible than I actually did, and now the teachings were strangely different than I had ever imagined. The conflict between what I was learning in the wilderness and what the Bible had to teach was beginning to resolve itself. It took Grandfather's purity of thought and his simplicity to clarify things.

I was so excited about what I had learned, and there were so many more questions spinning through my head, that I could not sleep. Instead I lay awake all night, thinking about the things of which Grandfather had spoken. I began to take the teachings I had learned from the Bible, and with each teaching I could clearly see the parallel to what I was learning from Grandfather. The more I dug into my mind, the more I understood. Though there were some teachings of the Bible that were technically different, when I looked at them as a whole, they were more similar than different. I wondered how many other religions, philosophies, and beliefs had been misunderstood throughout time. If what Grandfather had said was true, then there were things that bound all basic beliefs together. I wondered why man had not set aside his differences and especially why man could not see the common bonds.

I must have fallen asleep near sunrise, for I awoke with a start, yet picked up my last series of thoughts with ease. I immediately asked Grandfather a question, practically before I was fully awake. "What are the differences in all the various religions?'' I asked. I know now that Grandfather's reply was borrowed from the yoga tradition, but neverthe-less it made its point. Grandfather said, ''There was a man who was walking in the woods one bright and beautiful day. As the man walked, he discovered a sorcerer sitting quietly on a rock in a distant clearing. He knew that if he captured this sorcerer, the sorcerer would have to grant him a wish, so the man decided to stalk the sorcerer and try to capture him.

''The man walked quietly through the woods and into the clearing, approaching the sorcerer from behind. The man guessed that the sorcerer must be asleep not to have heard him coming, and that surely was the case. The man quickly slipped a rope around the sorcerer's body and wres-tled him to the ground. The sorcerer awoke, startled and a little ashamed that he had not heard the man coming. The man laughed and told the sorcerer that he would only gain his freedom if the would grant him a wish. The sorcerer thought for a moment and, realizing that there was no other way to gain his freedom, agreed to give the man his wish. They both agreed, and the man let the sorcerer free.

''The sorcerer then asked the man what he would wish for, and the man thought long and hard. Being a smart man, he did not want to wish for food, for he would only eat it and get fat. He did not want to wish for money, for he would only spend it on foolish things. So the man asked to be given a demon that would do his bidding for the rest of his life. This demon had to be powerful, do whatever the man wished, and obey his every command. Now the sor-cerer, also being very smart, agreed to give the man his demon. However, there was one stipulation. The demon would have to be kept busy all the time or it would devour the man, steal his spiritual consciousness, and remove him from the rapture of life. The man just laughed and said that it would be no problem, for he had many things for the demon to do. With that the sorcerer disappeared with a mocking sort of laughter.

"The man wandered back to his home, and when he walked in the door, his demon awaited him. Immediately upon seeing the man, the demon began to torment the man, begging for something to do. The man asked the demon to build him a house and completely furnish that house with the best of furnishings. The demon disappeared out the door, and the man, being very tired, decided to rest. No sooner had the man lay down than the demon returned and told the man that he had finished his task. The man was startled, for the demon had finished so quickly. As the man thought about what else to have the demon do, the demon began to banter the man, not giving him a moment's peace.

"Out of tormented desperation the man cried out to the demon and asked him to heal his dying friend, thinking that it would keep the demon busy for a long time. No sooner had the man uttered the words than the demon said that it had been done. With each new task the demon just uttered that it was done. The faster the man came up with new chores, the faster the demon completed them. Then it came to a point where the man could no longer think of things for the demon to do. As the man tried to think, the demon grew larger and began to take over his mind. The man felt himself begin to slip from consciousness, reality became distorted, and his tormented soul ached. In desperation the man jumped from the window and ran terrorized through the woods, until he finally lost the demon.

"The man ran down the trail, fearing for his life. He ran so blindly that he ran right into a shaman and fell to the ground exhausted. He saw the shaman standing over him, immediately crawled to his knees and begged the shaman to help him. The shaman patiently listened to the man's story, nodding his head in understanding. When the man finished, the shaman simply smiled and told the man that everyone has a demon. With that the shaman pulled a hair from his curly head and handed it to the man. He told the man to give it to the demon and tell the demon to straighten the hair. The man could not believe that something as simple as a hair could quiet the demon, for the demon could do all things quickly and easily. Before the man could say a word to him, the shaman was gone.

"The man began to walk home, holding the hair firmly in his hand. Suddenly the demon jumped from the brush and began to badger the man again. Sheepishly and reluctantly the man handed the hair to the demon and told him to straighten it. With a thunderous laugh the demon grabbed the hair, held it in his hands, and pulled it straight. As the demon let go of the hair it curled back up and the demon tried again and again but could not straighten the hair. With that, the demon shrank and stopped bothering the man. Seeing this, the man grabbed the hair from the demon and told the demon to carry him home. Once home, the man returned the hair to the demon, who continuously tried to straighten it, and the man lay down in a deep, profound sleep."

Grandfather just sat there when he finished his story with that smirk on his face that said, "Well, ask me the question."

I looked at Grandfather, now more confused than ever, and asked, "What the hell is the demon?"

Grandfather answered, saying, "Why, your mind, of course! The uncontrolled, logical mind, that badgers man all the time and allows him no peace."

"Then what is the hair?" I asked.

"You already know what the hair is. The hair is ceremony, custom, tradition, chant, songs, religious items, and even religion. It is anything or any object that quiets the logical mind so that the spiritual self can emerge. Many consider the hair to be a meditation, the ultimate quieting and purifying of the mind. It is the hair that constitutes the major difference between all religions, for the basic truths are the same.''

I was absolutely shocked by Grandfather's words. Could it be so simple? Is it then that all the basic truths of religion are the same and that the differences are only the hair? The hair was the vehicle that causes the person to arrive at the basic truth, thus quieting the logical mind so that the spirit can be reached. Then why, I thought, was there not just one hair for all people?

Grandfather's words broke into my thoughts, saying, ''Because there are many different kinds of people, there are many techniques, or hairs, that will work only for them. As man tries to complicate the simple truths, then all the hairs become complicated as well. When man can go back to the simple and pure truth, then he will need no hairs. The spiritual mind can then be reached in a pure and simple way, the way that Nature teaches.''

This concept and explanation was so simple and easy that at first I could not accept it. I had to walk for much of the day to think. As I began to look at my own life in the wilderness, I found that the wilderness had become a hair to me. As I looked into other religions and philosophies, I began to understand all the various hairs and how they were the primary differences in all these beliefs. If I could get beyond all the hairs, then I would arrive at the basic truths in all religions. But, I thought, that would take the better part of a lifetime to accomplish.

It was then that I realized that is exactly what Grandfather had done. He was a student of all philosophy, and his main mission in life seemed to be to simplify things. In the years that followed, he would frequently teach and quote from all manner of religions. Taoism would be interspersed with quotes from the Buddist faith, Christianity quoted along with Hinduism. There seemed to be no limits to his knowledge or his curiosity. But one simple fact remained, as it remains in me today. With all of his knowledge and all of his travels, he still came back to the simplicity and rapture of the wilderness. For it is in the wilderness where the fires of the spirit are born, and it is the common ground of all beliefs.

7

The Forty-Day
Vision Quest

For anyone constantly seeking to walk a spiritual path, there
is not one Vision Quest. Instead the quests are many, frequent, and vary in time and place. After the first Vision
Quest other quests remain unplanned by the logical mind.
Instead the subsequent quests are directed by one's spiritual
mind. Sometimes the spirit directs us to take a quest immediately, and at other times it gives us a time to plan. In
this way, by allowing the self to be open to the spirit, we
can be in immediate connection to the world of Vision, for
it is from the Vision Quest that we get our greatest guidance. We receive directions and answers from the world of
spirit in a pure way. By fasting and praying in a confined
area, the distractions of man are transcended, and the mind
becomes pure and is spirit.

It is in the Vision Quest that new directions are given or
the full wisdom of past quests revealed. Most of all, what
the Vision Quest does is to allow the inner self, the spiritual
self, to emerge. It is where we find out what we should be

doing in life, and it reveals the heart's greatest desires. Besides life in the purity of the wilderness, the Vision Quest remains the single most important tool that we possess. It holds all the answers. As Grandfather had so often said, it is the way in which we allow the physical self to sleep and to allow the spirit self pure time to speak to the Creator and to the Earth. Not only does it reach to the deepest desires of the heart, but also it teaches us what the Creator wants us to do. It teaches us to work for the higher self.

For the ten years I spent with Grandfather and for the ten years I spent wandering, I took at least four Vision Quests a year. Some of these quests were very short, lasting only one or two days. Other quests lasted much more than the required four days. Four times in my life I took a Vision Quest of forty days or longer, and it is of my first forty-day Vision Quest that I write now. That quest was to be one of the most important Vision Quests in my life, for it became the major directional force of my life. It is from that quest that my life has been guided down the path that I now walk. It is the quest that also told me that someday I had to leave the wilderness and go back to the world of man.

Why forty days, I do not really know. All I know is that the time and place were directed by a force outside myself. It could be that during the time of the quest's direction, I was studying the life of Christ. I was fascinated that He, too, took a Vision Quest for forty days. As I studied other philosophies I found that a period of forty days seemed to hold something special. Even going back to the time of Noah, it had rained for forty days and nights. I still have a deep desire to go to the same wilderness as Jesus and take a forty-day quest. Deep inside I feel drawn, for that quest holds so much wisdom. At this point in my life, in the earliest planning stages of such a quest, I still feel unworthy. I still have so much to learn.

I was in the summer of my fourteenth year when the direction of the forty-day quest came to me. It was still early summer, and I was buried deep within a Vision Quest. At this point in my life I had completed nearly twenty Vision Quests and had yet to receive the Grand Vision I had heard Grandfather speak of so often. This quest had been more miserable than any of the others. For nearly four days I had sat in that confined circle praying. More than ever, the Earth and creation remained silent. Nothing spoke to me, nor was I able to communicate with the Creator. I felt that my prayers had fallen to the Earth and that everything had turned its back on me. I was growing frustrated, as I had felt so often, filled with feelings of unworthiness and self-doubt.

As I waited for the sunrise of the fourth and final day I fell into the first deep sleep of my quest. As I awoke, I saw that it was still dark and that nothing had changed, except that I was not so paranoid anymore. I felt clear and whole. It was then that I realized that I was no longer being watched. For some strange reason it felt like I had passed some sort of test, though I did not know how or why. I felt so awake and alive. The dark landscape took on a purity I had never known. I had the feeling one gets when one has just finished a difficult project, that feeling of success, accomplishment, and a sense that a huge burden had been removed from my back.

As the dawn cracked the distant horizon, I gazed to where the sun would eventually rise, and watched as the sky grew brighter. As the sun's first rays cut deep into the dark landscape, I gasped in disbelief. The landscape was not that of the Pine Barrens but one that I had never known. All around were craggy rocks and boulders, sparse vegetation, and hot sand. The landscape looked stark and barren.

Even before the sun was up, I could feel a dry, oppressive heat, much like that of an oven. The wind began to blow with a hot and furious breath, moaning through the crags of rock and hissing on the shifting sands. There was no doubt in my mind that I was there, for it did not feel like a dream. I could feel all the sensations of this place and had complete control over my body. At least I thought I had control, until I tried to stand and walk and found that I was pinned to the ground.

It was then that I was drawn by a force more powerful than I had ever known. It compelled me to look directly at the sun, which practically burned my eyes from my head. I could feel the sun burning my face, to a point where my lips were blistered. Standing in the sun, as if totally composed of light, was a man. He had long flowing hair and white robes. Amazed, I thought it must be Jesus. My mind came rushing back and critically berated my thoughts. There is no way this man could be the Christ, I thought. I am but scum, and only those more worthy than I could receive those Visions and communications.

As I looked back at this man composed of light, a voice came from the land and spoke to me in a very direct way. The voice said, "The Bible teaches us all to be like Jesus. We must live a life as Jesus lived, and we must follow Him. Many scholars believe in this, yet why do they not seek to follow Jesus into the desert for forty days? Was that also not an example, a teaching, and a command? The reason most do not follow him there is that it is too difficult. What, then, will *you* do? Will you ignore this teaching or will you do what He has commanded you and so many others to do? You can no longer turn your back on this quest, for by doing so, you will deny your life and lose your Vision. It is only the Creator who decides if we are worthy, not our minds. Just accept that you have been watched, tested, and now chosen.''

The voice echoed the word *chosen* until it resounded in my head, and I awoke to the power of the Pine Barrens, saying that word over and over to myself. It all had been a dream, though a vivid and powerful one. I felt that it had come from all the study I was doing into the life of Christ and many other prophets of the past. I hurried back to camp, deep in thought. There could be no way I would ever be chosen for anything, for I was just a child in the things of the spirit. Jesus, if it was He, wouldn't consider a person who was not worshiping in a church every Sunday, I thought.

Grandfather sat in camp awaiting my return. As I approached him, he looked deep into my eyes, scrutinizing me every moment. Without hesitation I told him about my Vision Quest, how it had given me nothing but a very bizarre dream. I related the dream in great detail to him while he sat listening intently. After I finished the story I commented, in a mocking sort of way, that my mind must have created this illusion, for surely I could not be chosen for anything.

Grandfather smiled and said, "If this dream lacks truth, then why is your face so badly sunburned and your lips cracked and blistered? Today is the first sun we have had in five days, and it was only up for a few minutes. Grandson," he continued, "it is not we who decide if we are worthy to be chosen. It is the Creator's choice, and those who feel they are worthy will never be chosen. You must begin to make preparations for your forty-day Vision Quest, as you have been commanded to do. For you now have no choice."

Part of the preliminary preparations for my quest was to think through thoroughly the previous Vision. Certainly it was not Jesus who had approached me in that Vision, for

I could not be worthy of that. Visions like those were meant only for the powerful people, people who could make change and had the drive to see their Vision through. Grandfather may have been worthy to see Jesus, but not me. Spiritually I was just a child. I decided that it was enough for me just to have been approached by a spirit that looked like Jesus, for that was direction enough. Anyway, living in the woods and living the philosophy of the Earth was not strictly in the teachings of Jesus, so logically He would not have come to me.

Grandfather's voice again broke into my thoughts. "It makes little difference as to who or what the spirit was who came to you that morning. It is the message given that is important. Your heart knows the one who came to you, but your logical mind, society's mind, cannot accept this."

I said, "My heart then perceives it as Jesus, and I feel Him."

"Then if that is what your heart says, it becomes your truth. But again, do not concern yourself over the one who bears the message. Instead follow the direction of the message.

"You told me that you felt you were being watched. That your mind and body were laid open for all to see and you felt tested and tormented. This, then, is the reason for that long quest, for the spirits have looked into your heart, tested you, and found you worthy of this forty-day quest. They must be ready to teach and guide you, for you have been chosen as a result of that testing, for one quest to drive you to the next in such a powerful way. The communication and direction must be very important. So think no more of the one who sent the message, just prepare, and prepare quickly. I sense an urgency, and time is growing short."

As I began to wander the landscape searching for the place of the quest, my mind still ruminated over all the

events of my last quest. I felt deep inside that I wanted to
quest in a barren, hot, and dry area, much like the one I
had seen in my Vision. On and off over the next several
weeks I searched so many areas of the Pine Barrens, but
nothing felt right in my heart or my inner Vision. Several
times I came to an old gravel quarry that had been abandoned for quite some time. Each time I gazed across the
barren landscape my heart seemed to say it was right, but
my mind would not accept doing such a powerful Vision
Quest in something that had been manmade. So I continued
searching, desperately now, because I was running out of
time.

By mid-July I had still not found this special place and
had almost given up the whole idea. I thought that it could
be possible to do the quest in any of the areas I had chosen
before. I knew that there was no real desertlike area to be
found in these Pine Barrens. The only close one was the
gravel pit cut by man, but it wasn't pure and natural, as I
had wanted. By this time I was more than frustrated because the quest was to take place in four days and I hadn't
even found the area, nor began any of the prayers or preparations. I was beginning to think that the spirit world had
changed its mind and that for some reason I was unworthy
because I could not find the proper area.

Grandfather looked at me for a long time, and again my
thoughts felt so transparent and venerable. "In what area
does your heart feel good to take this quest?" he asked.

I told him about the abandoned gravel pit and how my
heart seemed to draw me there but that my mind wouldn't
accept the scars left by man as being pure and natural.

Grandfather stood and said, "Follow me!" And we both
walked down to the trail that eventually led to the gravel
pit. We did not talk, for I was too caught up in my own
thoughts and too curious as to what Grandfather was going

to do. The journey only took two hours, but it seemed like forever. When the mind reels with focused thought, time seems to stand still.

We approached the high lip of the canyonlike gravel pit and sat on that lip. All I could see was man's destructive power and how the landscape looked so sore with its deep and empty cuts. It was like man had gone in, slaughtered the Earth, and left her to die. I grew sick and disgusted. As the sun moved lower in the sky Grandfather gazed off across the huge, barren hole with a sense of rapture written on his face. Looking at him, I was confused. How could he find rapture in this sterile pit of rocky despair? He finally spoke. "What do you see, Grandson, when you look across this place? Yes, you see the scars of man, but can you look beyond those scars and into the real treasures and powers of this place?"

As I gazed across this broken land suddenly I saw its power and beauty beyond the scars of man. The glint and color of the stones seemed to glow with their own warmth. Tracks of life crisscrossed and wandered through every area of the pit. Deer could be seen on the edges, and near the center, on an old tree, perched a beautiful red-tailed hawk. Everywhere in the pit were signs of life that I hadn't noticed but were now becoming apparent.

Grandfather said, "You see only what you choose to see. Your heart saw the beauty, but your mind only saw the anger. So look beyond the mind and into your heart and you will see this place. It is this place that you have been directed to. It is your quest area."

We sat until the sun was well behind the horizon, showing only a fissure of light that partially illuminated the pit. For the first time I saw the pit as beautiful. Though man had scarred it, Nature's beauty was still there, and it beckoned me to the quest.

"Possibly," Grandfather said, "this is your final answer!" And he pointed off to a distant bank deep within the pit. I followed the direction of his point with my eyes, and there at the far end of the dump, partially hidden by the shadows, sat a man. I trembled as I saw his long white clothes and dark hair. I cried in prayer. How could I have been so damn stupid not to follow my heart? I looked up. Grandfather was walking back to camp, the man in white was gone, but my question had been answered.

For the next four days I attempted to prepare for this Vision Quest. The length of the quest really frightened me, for it would be the first quest I had ever taken that would have lasted for more than ten days. I was also upset because I could not understand why the spirits wanted me here or what they would try to teach me. I also fumbled with my preparations. I could not think clearly and was always shrouded in thought or analysis. I did not know what to pray for in the Sweat Lodge, nor did I really understand what I should be doing or saying in my morning and evening meditations. Even the animals and plants refused to hold conversations with me. The closer I got to the time I would have to begin that quest, the more alone I felt.

I awoke early on the appointed morning and the entire camp was deserted. Grandfather and Rick had vanished sometime during the night and taken all their things with them. Apparently they weren't coming back. Everything was quiet as I walked to the lip of the quarry. Even while trying to look through the world with the spiritual mind, things remained quiet, oppressively quiet, and at times frighteningly quiet. As I walked on, filled with fear, I could sense things moving out in the brush. I could also sense that these were not of flesh but of spirit. At this point the sensation of being watched and tested came hammering back into my mind. I had never experienced anything like it, not on any other quest. It seemed like many multitudes were walking with me to that same pit.

I finally got to the upper lip of the quarry, then traveled along to a pinnacle of earth that overlooked the whole pit. It was the farthest finger of land leading out to the center of the pit, barely ten feet wide on the top, sparse vegetation marking the point of the original ground, the walls nearly thirty feet high and vertical. It held a commanding view of the whole quarry and put me above its center. It felt so damn good to be there, but I sensed that many things watched me from the rims of the pit. Again the horrible sense of being watched and tested flooded me.

I sat quietly, staring off into the darkness. I could tell that it was near morning, but the distant glow hardly illuminated the pit area. I could see something moving in the distant shadows along the distant wall. By the way it moved and the shape of its body, I could tell that it was the "Stalker," of whom Grandfather so often spoke. Upon sensing its presence the hair on the back of my neck stood up straight and I could feel my heart pounding in my throat. A sickening feeling came over me as I caught its smell. As always, it was the smell of rotted flesh and death, a smell that always made my skin crawl and threw me into a panic. It was the beast I feared most in the Pine Barrens.

Grandfather said that we would encounter all manner of demons on our spiritual paths. Most of them we knew, for they came in the forms of self-doubt, distraction, and so many other negative emotions and thoughts. But there were demons, demons that were of evil spirits. These demons could cause confusion, injury, bad medicine, and even death. These were the same demons that had stalked man's mind and soul for as long as anyone could remember. Some were the same type of demon that Jesus threw out of the man in the temple. These demons became our most formidable enemy, for they fed on fear and self-doubt. Some could be confronted, but others had to be beaten. As far as I knew, this Stalker could not be confronted or beaten, such was his power. Grandfather said little about this one, avoiding the subject. The only thing he said was that one day I would have to face its power, and the confrontation would be my supreme test.

We had dealt with demons many times in our lives. They were not simple, ghostlike spirits but evil spirits with powerful missions. We'd seen them cause death and accidents; heard them screaming from the swamps and moaning in old buildings; caught glimpses of them wandering as tormented souls in abandoned graveyards. We had witnessed their blood sacrifices and watched them try to haunt the spirit areas of the woods, driving us away with screaming and evil laughter. They seemed to live in the fogs of man's mind, coming to flesh when the negativity and hatred or fear gave them power. At once they were real and dream, yet they could leave their mark on ground, tree, beast, or man. The line between reality and dream became thin, indeed. Fortunately they stayed to the evil areas, rarely coming out unless drawn to something spiritual that they wanted to destroy.

This one, the Stalker, seemed to be the most vile and powerful. He could turn any area bad, infecting the mind and soul with his hatred, and drive a spiritual person from his path. Now, for some reason, I could feel him there at the beginning of my longest Vision Quest. I was more frightened than I had been in a long time, but I was damned determined not to yield to that fear and run from this quest. It was too important, and nothing would drive me from this place. I was prepared to die here if that must be the case. With that thought the Stalker's presence vanished and the area was returned to full dawn.

Grandfather had said that it did not make any difference whether a demon was reality, dream, or imagined. A demon could inflict pain and suffering or distort thinking. Demons could drive a man from his spiritual path, or infect the mind and body with sickness and evil. Demons live in man's hatred and anger, and flourish in the dark side of the spirit-that-moves-in-all-things. They exist in evil and for evil, and wherever they go, in whatever they touch, there is evil. Demons are the dark side of man. When man was given a choice to seek good, evil, or complacency, that was the birth of demons. Thus demons were the spirits of evil and darkness.

The first ten days of the Vision Quest were a living hell. Again, it was as if Nature refused to speak and all of the spirits had turned their backs on me. I felt so alone, yet the feeling of being watched became so intense at times that I wanted to run from the quest area. The landscape was so barren and defiled by this huge gaping wound, inflicted by man. Everywhere I looked was pain and scars. Here the Earth seemed to be dead, the wound festering and deep, filled with pain. My emotions ran wild with hatred and anger, for man had done nothing to hide or heal the scars. Before me, like a constant reminder, lay that wound, always in my mind and sight, a monument to man's ignorance and disrespect.

The ridge I sat on was totally exposed to the elements and in plain view of everything. The sun beat my body during the day, and the chill winds of night caused me to shiver for hours. Each day seemed worse than the last, and each day my mind slipped more and more from the realities of life. Still nothing spoke, and the aloneness became oppressive and unbearable. In desperation I attempted to pray time after time, and still there was no response, not even from the heavens. This was more physical, mental, and emotional pain than I'd ever had to bear on any quest, and my spirit ached to be set free. But freedom was a myth, for my determination was a prison with no escape.

The nights were even more unbearable than the days, for it was the nights that produced the most bizarre hallucinations. The pain was worse at that time, for fatigue and darkness heightened the discomfort and distorted all thought. Shadows and sounds became harborers of demons. At night I felt even more vulnerable, weak, and relentlessly watched. Sometimes I felt a certain mocking persecution, where self-doubt flourished and fear became my ruler, the only reality. It was on the tenth night that I reached my limits and could bear no more. I stood to run from my terror and pain but fell into a place of nothingness.

I could feel my body and mind begin to slip away. Reality no longer existed and I could not think at all. I had the sense that I had awakened from a bad dream, but what I had awakened to, I could not comprehend. The world, my world, had changed. The pit lay before me as always, but all around things were different. The once lush Pine Barrens that had framed the edge of the excavation were now wilted and dying. There was no sound or motion. The air was thick with the smell of caustic chemicals and mingled with that of rotten flesh. As I looked to the sky the stars dripped great drops of blood that fell to the Earth with a searing and thunderous crash. The stars and the sky were red, blood red, and I grew so sick that I couldn't breathe.

I lay gasping at the edge of the pit, trying to get my breath and settle my stomach. It was then that I noticed that the entire floor of the excavation was covered with bodies. Bodies of humans, young and old, badly scarred, partially clothed, and almost fully rotted, lay from one end of the pit to the other. The stench was so sickening that it made my eyes water. The horror of it all terrorized my very soul, and the reality was too much to bear. I couldn't run; no matter how much I struggled to stand, I was held fast to the Earth.

I heard voices and the sound of light footfalls on the gravelly earth below me. A surge of hope welled up in my chest and I struggled to the edge again. As I looked down into the misty grayness of the pit I saw a line of children, stalking into the pit. As they went along they looked around carefully. Some held clubs, others held spears made from broom handles, all of them were sparsely clothed, very dirty, and terribly thin. They seemed frightened, yet they appeared to know what they were doing and where they were going.

I pulled back from the edge again and lay on my back, trying to clear my mind of this nightmare. It was then that I heard a crunching sound that drew my attention back to the edge. As I carefully peered over the edge I gagged at what I saw, barely able to control my stomach. The children were tearing at the bodies. Some of the children were feeding on limbs and fingers, others were feeding on the internal organs, and all were covered in rotted flesh, blood, and maggots. I could bear to look no more and pulled back from the edge again, unable to understand or even think.

The sound of a truck coming to the edge of the pit startled me. At the far end of the pit a huge dump truck was backing to the edge. I looked down to see if the children were still there, but they had vanished. I caught sight of some of the children hiding behind a large pile of bodies, watching as the truck approached the edge. It was obvious that they did not want to be seen. Suddenly the truck began to dump its load over the edge of the excavation. To my absolute horror the truck was dumping a load of bodies. These bodies looked even more emaciated than the ones in the pits. Apparently most of these people had died of starvation.

I watched the truck pull away. Armed guards stood on its sides as it slowly rumbled up the road, then disappeared in the dusty horizon. The children below me came out of hiding and cautiously began to make their way to the far end of the pit. Some of the children could not have been over six years old, with the oldest being about eleven or twelve. As they reached the pile of fresh bodies they began to feed on the flesh with a ravenous appetite. They seemed to care little that they were eating humans, nor did they let down their guard as they fed. They reminded me more of a pack of feral dogs feeding in a dump than a group of humans.

Suddenly a shot rang out from across the pit, and a young boy fell from the top of the body pile, blood pouring from his chest. Then another shot and another child fell, then another and another. The children ran through the body dump and up the distant bank, heads held low and zigzagging as they ran, which told me that they had been through this before. Four children lay dead on the body piles, and one wounded child in apparent agony was trying to crawl to safety. Another shot and the child was dead. My mind was so sick with horror that I was paralyzed, unable to even think of helping. The whole scene was so alien to me that I could not rationalize it, for now I was running almost purely on the instincts of the primal mind.

I watched as a group of men, dressed like bedraggled soldiers, stalked over to the edge of the pit. They scanned the pit and the walls, guns ready, as if at any moment they would be attacked. Finally three of the men entered the pit and headed for the dead children as the others stood guard. The men in the pit gutted the children, much like a deer hunter guts and field-dresses a deer, then pulled the children back up to the distant lip of the excavation. A strange four-wheel-drive vehicle, also camouflaged, entered the scene and a fire was started. The men now seemed more relaxed and began to joke around and talk loudly.

I watched them for what seemed like hours. They cooked one of the dead children on the fire and began to feast. The other children's bodies were tied onto the vehicle's hood, bumpers, and roll bar. I noticed that one of the men urinated into a can and passed the can to another, who drank it down. Just as they got into the vehicle and began to drive off, more shots rang out and the car crashed into a pile of bodies that lay on top of the ridge road. The children who had originally been in the dump had ambushed the men and had burned the vehicle. They collected all the guns quickly and returned to what remained of the Pine Barrens. The whole thing happened so fast that I could barely keep account of all the killing.

For the next several hours nothing moved. The stench of the rotting bodies and the caustic air was all that existed. It was then that I noticed that one of the men had only been wounded and now slipped quietly down the road. Instinctively I followed, cautiously watching the landscape for any movement. There were no animals, no birds, and no living plants. There wasn't any sign of water, and the only animal life seemed to be the persistent flies and carrion beetles. I followed the man for hours through the dead landscape as the air grew thicker with smoke and the caustic bite of chemicals.

In the distance I could see the rubble of a city, and I cautiously got as close as possible. The once proud city lay in ruin. The air was thick and more choking than back at the pit. People lay dying and bodies were piled along gutters. Some of the bodies had been eaten. Smoldering fires held the remains of charred human bones, and people drifted around in the littered streets as if in a daze. I passed what appeared to be a store, and hanging from hooks were parts of human bodies. People seemed to be buying these as one would a side of beef. Canisters of what looked like murky water lay at the back of the store, watched over by an armed guard. Everywhere was suffering, death, and the most vile pollution.

I wandered the streets in a daze, too numb to think or react. I realized that these people could not see me, for I was a ghost from the past and not of their world. The more I wandered and saw, the more I cried. Surely I knew that this would become the possible future that the prophecies spoke of. As I began to walk back in the direction of the pit an old man approached me, apparently able to see me. His face was drawn, full of oozing sores, his body frail with starvation. He looked me right in the eye and screamed in a feeble voice, "Why have you done nothing? Why have you sentenced me to this living hell?" He paused, looking into my eyes for a long time, then said, "Is this the legacy you have left for me, Grandfather?" Then I awoke back at the edge of the excavation. All had returned to my reality.

I was so shaken from the dream or the Vision, I did not know which it had been. I was aware that a considerable amount of time had passed, for there was evidence of rain, and the trees had grown paler and drier. I could have been gone for a day or a month, I did not know, nor did I know where I had been or how I had gotten there. I vividly remembered that world of death, and especially the old man's words. Could this be my grandchild, or great grandchild, and what did he mean by my legacy? I surely was not responsible for any destruction of the cities or for the death of those children. Surely he did not mean me.

It was then that I remembered what Grandfather had told me. That we are all responsible, even those who run away are responsible, for we are all part of the spirit-that-moves-in-all-things. So then I was responsible for this and I had done nothing to prevent it from happening. I felt sick, for this old and frail man could have been my grandson, or anyone's grandson; it made no difference, for we are all family and all responsible. I again remembered his words. "What have you done? What have you done?" I again lost the reality of time and place and slipped back off into the abyss of emptiness.

To my horror I was back in that world of possible futures. I lay again at the edge of the pit, still strewn with bodies and filled with the vile stench. As I rose from the ground I looked across the pit, and on the distant edge sat the old man I had seen in the city. He appeared to be praying, as his position was bent toward the ground in an attitude of reverence. I stalked around the edge to where he sat, and as I approached him, he spoke to me again. Without lifting his head he said, "You do whatever you must, but you can never run away." With that he lifted his head, and there in front of him was a tiny seedling, his hands cupped lovingly around its leaves. He said again, "You do whatever you can, no matter how little you feel it may be." With that he vanished, and I returned to my place at the edge of the pit of death.

I sat for a long time trying to think and to put everything I had learned into some order. But the stench of death disallowed any clear thought. The horror of it all overwhelmed me. This was a place where nothing really existed. There were no plants or animals, and death was the only escape. The spirits did not even come to this world, for the battles now raged in the world of spirit, and this world had been long forgotten. Here the demons had won. Man's greed and hatred had finally been rewarded. This was the fruit of man's labors. These were the sins of man's grandfathers and grandmothers and the results of living a life chasing the false gods of the flesh. This was a world without spirit, without hope.

The call of a hawk sounded, and I looked up and across the pit. There on the far side stood a group of people, so unlike the ones in the city. These people were healthy, yet they carried no weapons, nor were their faces wrought with anger. Instead they glowed with an inner peace and an outward happiness. They met the old man, hugged and kissed him, and turned not to the city but to the wilderness. In them I could feel a hope, a new hope. As the destruction of man lay all around them I felt that they held the answers to a new tomorrow. Truly, I thought, these must be the children of the Earth. "It doesn't have to end this way," a voice said. I turned abruptly toward the voice. Standing before me was the man in white robes I had seen in the Vision that had driven me to this quest.

It was not Jesus, as I first suspected, but a young Native American dressed in white buckskin robes. Quilled onto the robes were various signs of the Earth, Spirit, and the Creator. As he stood before me I had the deep feeling that I somehow knew who he was, but I could not place his face, though that was also very familiar. I thought that I might have possibly seen his picture in a history book, but that seemed too farfetched. He seemed to possess a knowledge that caused him to glow, a knowledge that I so desperately wanted and needed. Around him seemed to be an aura of peace, and though he was quite young, it seemed to me that he was a shaman.

As he spoke, the distant sky rolled with thunder and the Earth trembled. He gave me no chance to speak but said, "You have seen the stars that bleed and witnessed the destruction of the possible futures. You have seen the sick and barren Earth, the hatred, the destruction, and the Vision of your grandchildren dying. You have seen the children feed upon the remains of the children and you have seen an Earth of no spirit or hope. This is not the possible future but the probable future, and all that you have seen will come to pass. You are responsible for this future. So, too, are all the rest. All those who have run to the mountains and wilderness to hide are responsible, like all those who chased the false gods of the flesh. There are no innocent, except for the children who die in this place.''

The spirit continued, saying,''The old man asked what you had done to prevent this, and you had no answer. Nor have you even thought to answer, for you have done nothing. For you, who has borne witness to this land of death, there can be no answers, for there can be but one question. When will you do something to stop this death? Only when you have worked to save the Earth and the grandchildren can you have any answers. Only when you no longer run away and hide can there be hope. To run and hide in wilderness is to be responsible for the death of the world. There can be no running away for those who love.''

"But what can I do?'' I asked. "I am only a child, a small and weak voice in a land that hears nothing but money and power.''

"You cannot change things by thinking about changing things. You must do something, not talk or dream. The only answers lie in teaching people and leading them back to the Earth and the spirit. All other methods of change are temporary and shallow. You can only change things by changing the hearts of man. Each man must change before society changes, for it is the individual that contributes to the society, the wars, the hatred, and the destruction of the Earth. So then, if enough men and women are reached, the course and destiny of the flock will change. To teach and to lead is to love.''

The spirit vanished into a violent flash of lightning, and the Earth trembled with the thunder. I was back in my own time and place, seated on the lip of the excavation and filled with the words of the spirit. I knew then that someday I would have to leave the wilderness and try to do something to change the probable future. For me there could be no running away, for I had to do something, no matter how small and feeble I thought my voice might be. I was ready and willing to give up my dreams of wilderness to live my Vision. I did not know how or when, but I had to follow that Vision, and that Vision would provide the way.

Through the flashes of lightning I could see another man approaching me, again wearing a white robe. I ran from the hill to meet the spirit in the pit and to thank him for his wisdom and for the truth. I stumbled before the spirit and fell, exhausted by the quest. I looked up into Grandfather's face, his buckskin robes white against the dark sky, and I saw the quillwork of Earth, Spirit, and the Creator. Crying, Grandfather said, ''Welcome to the Vision of Love, Grandson.'' And my forty-day quest was over, forever changing my life.

8

The Stalker

There is a world between reality and Vision where there is good and evil, a world of spirit and of demons. It is a world where it is hard to separate imagination from reality, for encounters with this world can sometimes leave lasting physical effects. Crossing paths with a demon, whether imagined or otherwise, seems real and valid, especially during the time of the encounter. The reality of it all lies in the results, and the results are sometimes so startling and vivid that there is no need to question them. The encounter forever changes your perception of reality and life.

I have witnessed and suffered too much to discount the world of demon and evil as imagined. For where there is good, there is also evil. Where there are spirits, there are also demons. One cannot believe in one without accepting and believing the other. To deny that the evil exists in any small part of the world of spirit is to deny it all. One cannot pick and choose the reality of the other world to suit his or her own needs, for denying that evil exists, does not make it go away. Ignorance, in this case, can destroy. The danger, as always, is to deny that these things exist, feeling that if one does not believe in them, they will disappear. It doesn't take belief to give these things power, for they exist within their own power. They do not need us to give them validity.

There was so much to understand after my forty-day Vision Quest that I had trouble sorting it all out. Wisdom such as this could not be savored or studied in the company of others. Distraction only produced a certain confusion and clouded events. After any spiritual endeavor it was always best to get off alone to sort things out. This way there was a certain clarity of thought, and the events could be relived in all their intensity. Grandfather told me, almost demanded, that I go off and camp alone for a few days, especially after such a quest. Reluctant, because I wanted the company, I went off alone.

I decided to camp in an area that we had used many times before. It was a place where the migrating Native Americans had frequently stopped on their way to the bays and the ocean. The area was laced with the worn paths of their migrations and rich with the spirit of the past. Most of all the area was pure and wild, untouched since those days, for not even the charcoal makers of Colonial times had ventured there. The swamps and streams kept most people out, and the area remained wild and free. It felt good to be there, for there were no signs of anything but the pure and natural. Thoughts could remain untainted in this place.

For the first two days in the camp area I wanted to keep myself busy and free of all thoughts of the Vision Quest. I concentrated mainly on my survival skills and in the building of a comfortable camp. I chuckled to myself at the thought of people thinking that a primitive camp was uncomfortable. Survival living is one of the most easygoing and relaxing ways of life in any environment. Grandfather used to tell me that if a survival situation became difficult or painful, it just meant that the survivalist's skills were lacking. Survival is like being in the Garden of Eden, a perfect existence, in balance and harmony with Nature.

My camp became a work of art, and the work became a mandala for clearing my mind. A survivalist is a tool of the Creator, working with Nature to make things better, creating a balance on the land. A survivalist's camp becomes part of the land, and when abandoned and scattered to the Earth, there is no mark of its existence. So, building the camp, as always, became a science and an art form, blending one's existence to disappear into the natural order of things. My living in this area was not benign, but beneficial to the land. I became part of creation's laws, and my mind was set free to wander.

Once my camp was built, my food stores filled, and all the work of survival finished, I was able to relax and enjoy the purity of aloneness. For those days I became timeless the way only being in survival can bring. I ate when I was hungry, slept when I was tired, and played to exhaustion. I had no one to please but myself. For even living in a primitive camp with Grandfather and Rick would always bring some sort of order. Here, in my aloneness, there was nothing but me and my desires to fulfill. I tracked until my eyes burned, explored until my muscles ached, and swam until I shivered in the August sun. I felt so alive, so pure, so free of all things. My world became perfect. My only regret was that so many others would never know this world.

During this time of physical rapture there was also spiritual renewal. For some reason it felt good to get away from the learning and searching process and practice what I knew. My relaxed world became a duality, of flesh and spirit, where there was no separation of reality from the world of spirit. I realized that even a person who wasn't inclined to seek spiritual things could not go to wilderness without becoming part of that world he denied. In the purity of a primitive camp there can be only believers, for the rapture of creation fuses with the soul.

There is a metamorphosis that takes over man's existence. It is a change in perception so that man can truly walk within the consciousness of Nature and spirit. Animals no longer run from one's approach, trees give freely of their knowledge, and waters pass through and cleanse the mind and body. There becomes no reality except this, no world outside this world of peace and tranquillity. Here prayer becomes real and powerful, where the connection from self to the Creator is dynamic and reciprocating. My life became one constant prayer of thanksgiving. I honored the Creator and Nature with each step, every action, all thought.

It became a joy to go to the river each sunrise and sunset, to meditate and pray as the events of the past day and night became clear and real. It was a time to reflect on life and love. All the things that had troubled me vanished. There was no longer confusion in the flesh or in the reality of Vision. There at the water's edge I found the truth, and the Vision of forty days became crystal-clear. With each passing day the Vision revealed more wisdom and understanding. I could feel its urgency, and I could feel a resolve within my mind and soul to work to save the Earth.

It was during my evening meditation of the fifth day that I was struck with a powerful sense of panic. I do not know what happened, but I was sitting by the water's edge when I began to feel uncomfortable. What overwhelmed me wasn't only a feeling of being watched but a feeling of dread. Certainly I'd had that feeling of being watched before, both by animal and spirit, but this feeling was penetrating and absolute. More than being watched, I felt like I was being stalked. Even the movements of Nature stopped, for there wasn't the sound of birds, wind, or water. Everything was still.

Just as quickly as the feeling overtook me, it was gone. However, it left a certain uneasiness that stayed with me through that night and well into the next day. Nothing felt the same for me. The feelings of aloneness and purity in the camp had vanished. I was no longer at ease and relaxed. My senses were on constant alert as my eyes searched every movement and shadow. My ears strained at every crack and unidentified sound. My Garden of Eden had turned into a battleground of mental torment. My attention was now rapt and urgent instead of flowing and steady.

That night came and went without event. Everything on a physical level remained the same, but the sense of urgent alertness never subsided. Even the rising sun gave no relief, even though the feeling of being stalked had long since vanished. I felt stiff and restricted throughout the day, as if each movement had to be carefully orchestrated. Instead of letting my senses expand to Nature, I found that I retreated within myself more frequently, to let my inner Vision check the movements that surrounded me. At times camp felt restrictive much like a prison. It was no longer a sanctuary but now a nemesis. I had lost much of what I had come here to find.

By mid-afternoon my mind and the consciousness of Nature seemed to return to normal, and I relaxed again. I did not try to reason the feeling that I had had, for many times an inner Vision does not lend itself to physical answers. I had learned long ago never to question that feeling but to obey it without hesitation, no matter how irrational it seemed. I began to get into the flow of aloneness again, no longer fearing to leave camp but exploring the cedar swamps without restriction. At day's end I again returned to pray by the water and began to think of my Vision. The cold hand of fear grabbed me again by the throat, sending me running back to camp in an insane panic.

I cranked on my bow-drill to make a fire, trying desperately to beat the setting sun. All around me I could feel a presence, watching and stalking. It filled me with a blind terror, causing me to fumble the coal time after time. Getting a fire started, something I could do in the pouring rain or blindfolded, became nearly impossible. My hands shook uncontrollably and the muscles in the back of my neck ached. I was nearly out of control with panic, and it took all of my resolve to keep from running blindly back to Grandfather's camp. I had not felt such fear and panic since I was a child and had had to face what I thought was the Jersey Devil.

Fire finally blazed and cut deep into the night. Shadows deepened and danced, refusing to give up their secrets. Every sound seemed to slice through my nerves, and every emotion was on edge. I did not even leave the firelight to urinate, nor would I climb into the dark recess of my debris hut. I was a prisoner of the fire and my own fears. I tried to reason, but reason was impossible. I considered the thought that it might be a dog pack stalking me, but the fear was so deep and intense that it reached beyond the flesh and tore at my soul. It was more than any dog pack or anything of flesh. It had to be evil from the world of spirit, certainly a demon.

The power of this thing, this demon, haunted me through the night. I would not move from the fire, nor would I give in to sleep. I could feel it moving just outside the firelight. I could feel it watching me, its gaze almost burning holes into the night. Most of all I could feel it stalking me, waiting for me to make a move or a mistake. Every part of my body, mind, and spirit was on full alert and strained for more vigilance than I was capable of. This struggle lasted the entire night and past sunrise. Yet again the feeling dissolved with the mists of morning, and I felt as if I could breathe again.

For most of the morning I searched around camp for any sign or track of that which stalked me. There was nothing. The Earth revealed no track or trace of anything out of the ordinary, except for the fact that the natural flow had somehow been altered, for no animals had come near my camp during the entire night. There had been no fresh animal tracks since the past evening. I was not perplexed or shocked by this, for it only confirmed my beliefs that this thing was from the other world. It had to be an evil essence, for animals never avoided any spirits but demons. Surely, I thought, this thing must have tremendous demonic power to drive all the animals away and to cast such fear into me. I normally couldn't be shaken that easily.

At first I wanted to leave camp but refused to give in to the feeling. I had seen too much in my life to be driven off so easily. My sanctuary had been invaded, and now I was angry. I did not know what this thing was or why it wanted to drive me from this place, but I would not give in to terror, real or otherwise. I felt that to give in and run would be a defeat that would haunt me for the rest of my life. I would not allow myself to be driven from the place I loved so much, or from my thoughts. Nor would I allow my aloneness to be cut short. For if I let it win now, then it would always win, and aloneness would forever be difficult.

For the rest of the day I forced myself to explore. I tried to pass out of my mind any thought of what had happened that past night. As the day progressed, I pushed myself farther out of camp and into the deepest recesses of the swamps. I swam in tranquil pools at the base of towering cedars, laid back, and looked at the sweep and wave of their lofty crowns. I lost myself in the mysteries of countless tracks, contemplated the colors of wildflowers, and listened to the symphony of birds. Slowly the purity of Nature began to cleanse me of all the terror and agony that I had lived through. I began to feel whole again, and my confidence returned. I fell into a much-needed sleep on a mossy bank deep within the swamp.

I awoke violently to a distant howling. All was dark. The thick mists rose on columns of invisible air, barely illuminated by a crescent moon. At first I was frightened and nervous, fearing that I was being watched again, but the sounds of the night drowned out all fear. I was at peace and back into the full consciousness of Nature. I lay for a long time, soaking up the purity of the swamp, listening intently to the chorus of frogs mingling with the voices of uncountable insects. I thought about this place and how pure it was compared to the outer world of man. I remembered my Vision and the pit of bodies and the children feeding on rotted flesh. Again I resolved to fight that destruction any way I could.

The night became absolutely silent—except for the occasional branch cracking, which threw me into an overwhelming panic. I sat up abruptly and felt its presence again. A stench of rotted flesh rose from the swamp and I could clearly hear a deep, hoarse breathing. It was back, stalking me, and now more than ever I could feel its presence, almost see it moving. My terror took over all thought and I began to run wildly through the swamp, desperately trying to make it back to camp. I crashed through brush, gouged myself on briars, and impaled myself on broken branches. I had to struggle hard to get through the thicker brush that tore at my flesh and held me fast. Several times I stumbled and fell, crashing into the thick muck of the swamp. The thing kept chasing me relentlessly, driving me into a crazed state of horror.

I ran from the swamp and back to the trail leading to camp. My body ached with deep cuts and I could taste the blood running in my mouth. The only sound was my pounding breath; all else was silent. Nearing camp, I tripped again, and fell facedown into something warm, wet, and bloody. In the moonlight, just beneath my face, I could see the mangled carcass of a dog, and with a new burst of energy and speed I ran right through camp. I had to get to Grandfather's camp, for I knew that my camp would hold no sanctuary. I could sense it watching me, stalking me, and driving me from the woods. I had been beaten, and a thousand screaming voices echoed through my head as I stumbled and fell into Grandfather's camp.

I awoke, flailing my arms in a panic and screaming. Hands fell onto my shoulders and I opened my eyes to daylight and to Grandfather's smile. Grandfather had taken care of my cuts and bruises and allowed me to sleep for a while. He did not have to question me, for he knew what had happened. When I felt a little stronger, he finally spoke. "You know that you have to face this demon they call the Stalker. Until you do, you will remain defeated and frightened. He tries to drive you from the consciousness of Nature and from the spirit mind. Most of all he tries to drive you away from your Vision. If you don't beat him, then your Vision dies. Now go, as soon as possible, for the longer you wait, the stronger he grows." With that Grandfather left his camp.

I lay for a long time thinking of Grandfather's words and of the terror I felt. Grandfather had been right. This demon, the Stalker, was trying to take me from my Vision and drive me from the wilderness. He had come every time I tried to think about my Vision or of spiritual things and had effectively distracted my mind. Right now he had won the battle, for I had abandoned my camp and I had been unable to face my Vision. I knew that I would have to go back and face him, for to linger here would be to accept defeat. He was already growing stronger, and the longer I waited, the more frightened I became.

Cut, bruised, and exhausted, I walked back to my camp. My mind ran wild with fear, but my determination and anger would not allow me to turn back. As I entered my camp the tranquillity of this place was destroyed, for my camp lay in ruin. My debreis hut had been destroyed, my fire scattered, and many trees broken. In my worship and prayer area, by the water, lay the carcass of the dead dog I had discovered the night before. The area had the stench of rotted flesh and the constant drone of flies feasting on the dog's carcass. Piles of excrement, the likes of which I had never seen, lay strewn about the camp, and those also reeked.

I spent the better part of the day rebuilding my camp. I buried the dog's carcass along with the other waste and stocked my woodpile. I cleaned my worship area and tried to set the place back in order. I was preparing for a long night and, if need be, a long battle. The more I cleaned, the more my anger festered, until I was more than ready to face whatever it was that had driven me from the area. I did not hate this thing, for I knew that hatred, like fear, was what it fed on. Anyway, it was a teacher, no matter how vile, and I had to learn what it had to teach.

Night came quickly, but I did not go to my camp and build a fire. Instead I sat in my prayer area and awaited full dark. I began to think deeply about my Vision and of the quest, as I had planned to do so many days before. As soon as my thoughts turned to fighting the destruction of man, the night became quiet again, and I could feel its presence.

Terror again overtook my mind, and I felt the panic rushing into my soul. Fighting the overwhelming feelings, I refused to give in, and I would not allow my thoughts to be distracted. Again and again the feeling of panic rushed in, but I did not yield.

This thing was relentless and began to try all manner of fear to drive me from this place again. Images rushed into my head and I fought them back. Strange smells and sounds filled the night, but I would not give in to their distraction. With each battle won, I found my resolve growing stronger and my mind clearer. This thing began to lose its power, retreating farther and farther into the swamp, until finally it was gone. The night was returned to Nature as I heard its stalking steps vanish in the night. I had beaten the Stalker, and the Vision was mine. I would not run from the wilderness or my Vision again.

I don't know why, but I had a strong urge to follow this thing. Though I wasn't sure which way it had gone, I suspected that it was at the far end of the swamp, for that is where I heard its last sounds. I began to pick my way through the swamp, being careful to avoid the thicker patches of bull briars, and was especially careful of the mud. All fear had left me now, and a feeling of triumph quickened my pace. Curiosity had gotten the best of me, and I desperately wanted to follow this thing. Possibly I would get a glimpse of it, or maybe even confront it again, thus making my victory certain and lasting.

Once out of the swamp I continued to follow the Stalker, not by sight but by inner feeling. I could sense his movements far ahead and feel his evil presence. Always he kept far ahead of me, as if now the roles had changed and I was hunting him. I followed him relentlessly, growing stronger and more confident with each passing mile. I knew that if I could only catch him or follow him to where he was, I could drive him from these woods forever. I was going to find him, even if I had to chase him right to the spirit world and destroy him there. I wanted him to pay dearly for my terror and especially for driving me from the woods like some frightened child. I felt like a warrior.

My path took me to areas of the western part of the Pine Barrens I had never explored before. I could feel him moving in the blackness far ahead, and almost out of sight. Wherever he traveled, there was always a pervasive silence that sliced into the night woods. At the places he lingered, there was always a stench of rotted flesh and a deep chill to the air. I kept my pursuit for miles, until finally I left the woods and entered an old, overgrown field. At one time it must have been part of a farm, for I could make out an old building at the far end of the field and a large shed or barn of some type.

I slowed my pace and headed for the structure, for that is where my gut feeling led me. I approached carefully. Often these old structures were used by stray dogs, especially this close to the landfills. As I stepped into the blackness of the barn my ears strained for sound, but all that spoke were a few mice. Slowly my eyes became accustomed to the darkness, and I saw shafts of the night sky through the broken roof. Silhouetted against the larger holes were meat hooks hanging from the rafters. Here and there were chains with other hooks. I had entered an old slaughterhouse.

Chains rattled at the far corner of the barn, and I nearly jumped through my skin. A cat let out a hideous cry, and my nerves grew still. The place had an awful feel to it, and the rattled chains and screaming cat didn't make it feel much better. I also knew that the Stalker had been here, for the place reeked with its odor. I pushed through thick cobwebs and out a back door leading to another overgrown field. It felt good to be out in the night again and free of that dusty old death house. Still I pressed on, more determined than ever to find this thing that haunted me.

Passing through the remains of an old picket fence, I thought that I had entered an area where an old farmhouse must have once stood. That was until I noticed a few old gravestones and some rusted wrought-iron figures. As I bent down to silhouette the figures against the sky I was horrified to find that they were not small cherubs as I had thought but gargoyles of some sort. Their mouths gaped open and I could see long tongues protruding beyond vicious fangs. Chills ran up my spine and I quickened my pace. I did not like the feel of this place.

I pressed on, driven by my obsession to find this thing. It had led me to areas of the Pine Barrens I had never known, and each place had been evil. I passed through another patch of thick woods and then into another clearing. This clearing made me sick and dizzy as soon as I entered its confines. It reeked of the Stalker, more than anyplace I had yet been, and I began to experience an uneasy feeling creep over me. Again I fought the feeling, beating back the fear, and walked to the center of the clearing.

The clearing was perfectly round, and near the center was a white patch of sand, also round. At its center was a pile of sandstone blocks, arranged like a table. Four rays of sandstone blocks came off the main table and reached to the edges of the sand patch. Nothing grew from the sand or the sandstone crevices, yet they seemed old. As I felt the sand there were no footprints or sign of any animal. The area felt more evil than I could handle, and I had to pause for a long time to regain my composure. This circle seemed to drain my energy and drive; I had to sit down.

As I sat at the edge of the sandstone table I noticed that it had a huge pile of sticks in its center. Reaching for the sticks, I found to my revulsion that they were not sticks but blackened bones. Even though they were old and crumbling, they were still recognizable. There were bones of dog, deer, cat, sheep, and many goats. I could also feel teeth in the pile of old ash. Unable to control my fear and muttering to myself that it must be an old cook table, I tried to walk to the edge of the sand circle, but my legs would not work. I had to crawl, my head dizzy, the dark landscape spinning, and I lost consciousness.

I don't know if I had entered some dream or a bizarre reality, but I awoke to the flicker of a fire on the sandstone table. It was no cook table but an altar of some sort. Cloaked in the shadows of darkness at the far end of the sand circle was a dim figure, its hands, grotesque and animal-like, lifted to the sky. The feeling of evil was now so powerful that I could think of nothing else. Terror came rushing back into my consciousness, but my scream seemed frozen in time. I felt the evil of this thing, this black shaman, begin to seep into my mind, and I tried desperately to fight its power.

All my energy seemed drained and dissipated. I felt like I had been mortally wounded, and my essence was pouring into the rotted sand and being eagerly swallowed. I felt my mind flicker in and out of reality. The figure at the far end was growing larger, clearer, and more menacing. It was then, in a flash of clear consciousness, that I realized that I had been lured here. The Stalker, that thing, had beaten me again. It had effectively removed me from thoughts about my Vision by beating me at my own game. It had used my own anger to beat me and to lead me to this trap of evil. I felt so defeated and humiliated.

Now, fully realizing that I was again the hunted, I struggled desperately to leave the area. I could not move my body and felt pinned to the ground. It was a suction, holding me there, taking my will. I was held fast. The more I struggled, the more I became paralyzed. My hatred grew and I continued to struggle but to no avail. The ground seemed to feed on the hatred and my struggle. I almost gave up hope and was about to give in to whatever it was that wanted to take me.

I felt the sand pressing against my flesh as the ground pulled me closer. It was at this moment, while feeling the sand, that I felt sorry for this ground. It had been defiled, like a scar of evil on the Earth. If I could only give up my life for this ground, I thought, then my life would become worthwhile. With that thought the ground seemed to give up its grip and I could move. I realized then that this evil place repelled thoughts such as this. I began to pour out love to the ground and to all the hideous evil that surrounded me. With that the ground released its grip, the flame flickered, and all was gone.

I staggered from the field, totally disoriented and thoroughly drained. Not only was my body badly beaten, but so, too, was my spirit. It was the first time in my life that I had felt so spiritually beaten. I staggered as I moved back through the graveyard and passed the old slaughterhouse. It wasn't until I hit the familiar trail that I regained some strength. All the while something followed me, something stalked just outside of sight. My mind could no longer fight, and I just kept pressing on toward camp.

With each passing mile the Stalker's presence became more oppressive. The fear again rose within me, and my thoughts were close to panic. As I neared the swamp that bordered my camp I plunged into its depths and began to struggle through the thick brush and muck. With each step I felt the demon coming closer, trying to drive me away from my camp and back to Grandfather. I could no longer contain my fear and panic. I ran blindly for a few yards, then crashed right into a deep pit of mud. I sank up to my chest.

I heard a distant mocking laughter and the howl of dogs. This thing had won another battle, and I was about to perish in the mud because of my own stupidity. It was then that I decided to fight this thing with every bit of strength I had. As far as I was concerned, I would rather die in this muck than be driven from the woods or from my Vision. A shrill scream broke the silence and I heard a distant running. The sounds of the swamp returned to normal and was once again at peace. I was so exhausted that I could barely crawl from the mud to lie on the mossy bank and fall asleep.

I awoke in my prayer area to the sounds of birds and a glorious sunrise. I was covered in dried mud, but the whole episode seemed a dream. My tracks from the night before ended here in this sacred area. Exploring for most of the morning, I found no evidence that I had traveled beyond the stream that cut through the swamp. The dream, or the spiritual reality, had been so vivid that I could not tell where reality ended and my dream began. All I knew was that somehow I had beaten the Stalker again. It didn't feel like a victory but more like a standoff, one of mutual respect.

I wandered for much of the day, trying to piece together the events of the past night, the past week, and ultimately the past month. It was all difficult, and many things are not to be understood in this reality. The important thing was that I had learned from this dream, the forty-day Vision Quest, and from this camp. It made little difference how I learned, for the lessons were powerful. I felt free again and at peace. The good medicine of this camp area had returned and grew within me. I was home, and the Vision was mine once again.

I sat for a long time in my medicine place near the water.

I thought again of my Vision and of all the splendor of the spirit world. I could feel the Stalker lurking in the darkness, but I ignored his power. For a while he tried to steal my consciousness, but I continually ignored his presence, until he finally slipped away into the abyss of the night. He could no longer harm me, nor I harm him. Each of us lived in our own worlds. He would try to drive men from their Visions and I would try to lead men to those Visions. However, there could never be peace between us, for now we stalked each other.

I stayed at my camp for a few more days to make all that I had learned manifest. Sometimes you can fight evil and beat it and sometimes you can only keep it in check. I learned never to feed evil with evil, nor hatred with hatred, nor to fight fear with fear. I learned to fight with love for even those things that I despised. When I returned to Grandfather, he simply said, "It is not important what you believe is dream and what is reality. For what is important is that you learn, and what they have to teach."

9

The Robe

I had remembered the robe that Grandfather had worn during the forty-day Vision Quest. I never asked him about the robe, for I felt that it was very personal to him and probably sacred. I did not often ask him about sacred items; if he wanted me to know, he would eventually tell me their significance, their power, and their meaning. I had remembered seeing the robe worn by the young Native American who directed me on my forty-day Vision Quest, and I remember seeing the man in a robe again, several times during that same quest. Then, finally, Grandfather came to me in that same robe when my forty-day quest ended. I knew that it had to be significant and special for me, for it had appeared so often.

I remember it vividly. It was made of old brain-tanned buckskin and had been deeply smoked. It was then covered in white clay to make it pure white. On what would be the lapels were symbols of the Creator, the Earth, and the sky, as well as symbols of all the teaching directions. Some of the symbols were painted on, others were of quill design, and others were beaded. There was also a light fringe to the hem, and the garment seemed very old and well worn. Whenever I encountered it in my Visions, dreams, or thoughts, I was awed, always deeply curious.

It wasn't until almost a year after I last saw the robe in my Vision that I could finally understand its significance in reality. My first real physical encounter with the robe came without my realizing I was meant to encounter it. Essentially I was set up by Grandfather and lured to its power. I realized now that Grandfather could never explain the robe to me but that I had to find out for myself. It was something that could only be understood through the heart.

I had gotten a long weekend off from school for some sort of fall teachers convention, and planned to spend the full four days in the woods practicing my skills. It had been a year since my first forty-day Vision Quest, and I still had much to digest and work out. The four days alone would give me much-needed time away from Rick and Grandfather to practice what I knew. On that long weekend Grandfather had gone south to visit old friends, and Rick had gone with his father for the weekend on a trip. I had all the new lessons I needed for a long time, and I was eager to get started mastering many of them.

I arrived in camp just as Grandfather was packing the few medicinal plants he needed to take with him on the trip. One of his friends was sick, and the plants would help him immensely. I helped Grandfather pack and made sure the plants were in good order. He hardly spoke a word as we worked, except to ask me what I planned to do that weekend. I told him I was going to practice many of the skills I had learned during the summer and that I was also going to use the quiet time to work on the wisdom of my Vision Quest. He smiled and said, "Go without expectation, for expectation can become a rut that will keep you from your real path of learning.'' He paused for a moment, then said, ''I have left something for you to look at in my lodge. See that you return it when you are done.'' With those words he disappeared down the trail.

At first I wanted to go and see what Grandfather had left for me, but I was running late and still had to set up my camp. I had to gather food and other materials if I wanted to get right down to practice in the morning. I decided to let my curiosity pass and set up camp. The process of setting up camp, building a fire, getting food and the other materials for my practice took up most of the afternoon, and by the time I could relax, it was already too late to work on any skills. I was a little disappointed about not being able to get at least something done that evening.

I crawled into Grandfather's lodge to find out what he had left for me, but the lodge was dark. As I groped around in the dark an eerie feeling came over me. It was the same feeling of being stalked and watched that I had experienced when I'd encountered the Stalker. Though I had grown to ignore its presence, it still bothered me greatly when he was around my camp. As I came out of Grandfather's lodge I could feel his presence stronger than ever, to a point where I could no longer ignore him. I began to search around camp, but the feeling came and went periodically. Now, free of the Stalker's presence, I went to sleep.

The next morning I awoke angry, for I had understood why the Stalker was around the camp. I felt that his presence was a distraction to keep me from practicing my skills as I had planned. I immediately set to work, building an Apache water basket, for that was a skill I wanted to master. I had built several baskets, but I was not as fast and efficient as I wanted to be. Periodically as I worked, I could feel its presence again and again, but I would not let it distract me from my work. The whole day and part of the night passed by in that way, until I put away the finished basket and the presence was gone. I was determined not to let this thing get to me again and distract me from my work.

After eating, I relaxed by the fire to sort out various parts of my Vision Quest. Again I felt the Stalker's presence just outside of camp, stronger than ever. Now there were sounds and other disturbances that went along with the feeling of being watched. They were certainly not the sounds of Nature but the grunts and moans of the underworld. The area was also at times filled with wafting mists that reeked of rotted flesh. Several times I felt myself becoming angry, but I knew that anger and hatred would only feed the Stalker's soul. I continued on as best I could.

As the night grew late and I began to hit the wall of mental and physical fatigue, I put away all thought of my Vision Quest. The Stalker was gone. I sat for a long while relaxing, almost asleep, when I remembered that Grandfather had left something for me. As soon as I rose to walk to the shelter the stench of the Stalker returned. It was so harsh that it made me gag, and my eyes began to burn and water. Anger filled me, and I could feel the Stalker grow in power, as if feeding on me like a leech. I again passed it out of my mind and went to the water to wash out my eyes and to get away from my anger. The night was peaceful again, and I decided to sleep by the water.

The whole next day was quiet as I tracked out of camp, following the trail of a mink. I remained unmolested through the morning as I followed the mink deep into the swamp. The mink led me through bogs and waterways, over logs, and through the muck, finally ending in one of Grandfather's old Vision Quest areas. At the far side of the sacred circle the mink fed on a small fish, and for the next few moments I stalked to get close to him. He finished the fish and bounded off into the bush at the far side of the swamp. I entered Grandfather's quest area after praying, something I would not normally do. Yet something called me here. As I looked around I found one of Grandfather's old direction poles, and in its center was his symbol. The symbol interpreted as "Things are not what they seem."

I felt as though I were being given a subtle message, as if the mink had led me to the quest area and Grandfather had purposely left the stick for me to find. I thought about this all the way back to camp but could not see how it would fit into what I was learning here and now. At camp I began to think about the ways I could bring my Vision to other people. I knew that modern man looked at a person with a college degree or a title of status as having power and a person to be listened to. I had neither, nor did I ever care to go to college, into politics, or into business where I would have an influential title. I was afraid no one would ever listen to what I had to say. At least not without having the power that they respected, and I loathed that kind of power.

I also knew that people did not like to be preached to. People, and even me, hated anything to do with preaching. I knew that petitioning, demonstrating, and even rioting would have little impact. There had to be a way to reach people in such a way that you opened their hearts, changed their thinking, and came back to the reality of the Earth. People had to be reached at the level of their hearts, not through their minds. I could see no way that it could be done, especially if I had to do it myself. I just didn't get along with people, avoiding crowds whenever possible. I did not see how I was going to reach anyone.

I fell asleep with these thoughts and questions rushing through my head. The Stalker had left me alone for much of the day and night, and all seemed to be at peace. I had a great night's sleep, deep and dreamless. I awoke the next day and decided to take a walk out of camp and collect some small stones of quartzite that I would make into arrowheads. The best quartz and gravel beds lay in an old sand pit that was very close to civilization, but they were usually free of people. I needed those stones, anyway, if I wanted to practice the new arrowhead-making technique Grandfather had shown to me in late summer.

I slipped to the edge of the pit, concealing myself under some old root systems. I wanted to make sure that no one was around that I would have to talk to. When I saw that the pit was free of human tracks and that no one was around, I slipped into the smaller of the two pits and began to collect stones. I had been collecting for nearly an hour and had some fine stones when I heard a truck coming into the larger pit. Like the animals, I ran and hid in the upper root systems.

As the truck's motor was shut off, I heard a door open and close. Apparently only one person was in the truck. Then I heard the hood open and distinctly heard the rattle of tools. Possibly, I thought, this person had broken down and was attempting to fix his truck. I worked my way around the pit as the work on the truck continued, and within a short period of time I had a good view of what was going on. It was a pickup truck, all right, and the hood was open. Underneath the truck I saw the legs of its occupant, apparently working on something.

I thought that this would be a great opportunity to test my scout skills and see how close I could get to the truck. I worked my way down the edge and into the thick brush that bordered the lower part of the cliff. I knew that from here I would have a clear view of the driver and could see what he was doing. The area would also afford good protection. As I pushed through the brush and looked at the truck I was horrified. The driver was changing his oil and draining the old oil right onto the ground. I had to fight back the anger that seemed to consume my every thought. Within the next half hour he had used cans of oil and his old oil filter thrown on the ground.

I could take no more and emerged from the brush. I walked toward him and got to within a foot of him before he noticed me. He jumped and assumed a defensive stance, waiting for me to attack or run. I said, "Nice truck," emphasizing the word *truck*. He then dropped his guard. He was amazed that I was so far back in the bush, for he, too, used the wilderness as an escape. He loved to hunt and fish and especially to get away from people. We talked for quite some time, especially about hunting, fishing, and the woods. My anger began to subside as I realized that this guy did not mean to pollute the Earth, he just knew no better. He had been raised in a city and was only beginning to learn the way of the wilderness.

As we spoke, I was beginning to teach him things about the woods that he had not known, and his attitude seemed to be changing. I asked him if he wanted to catch some big pickerel or bass, and he immediately said yes. He grabbed his fishing pole from the back of the truck, and we walked a short distance to a hidden pond at the edge of the excavation. He was surprised, because his truck was so close to the pond, yet he hadn't seen it because of the high brush. As we neared the edge and he looked across the pond, I could tell that he was stunned by its beauty.

I told him to cast his line just a few feet from the bank and a few inches to the outer edge of a submerged cedar log. As soon as the lure hit, the water seemed to boil, and a good-sized bass took the hook. He fought the fish for a few minutes, taking care not to break his light line. I could see his hands trembling in excitement as he landed the fish on shore. Though he had lived near the Pine Barrens for a few years, this was the largest bass he had ever caught. He was so excited, he could barely talk, and he even tripped a few times on the way back to the truck. He could not thank me enough.

He put his pole away and set about cleaning the fish on the tailgate of the truck. I told him then that he should catch as many fish as he possibly could, because this pond would not be producing fish for much longer. I had no idea where the words were coming from, for it was like my body and mind were moved with a force outside of myself. At the same time I could feel the Stalker watching us, though the guy seemed to take no notice. I felt that possibly he was still in a logical frame of mind and not yet in the spirit mind. He had not been in the woods long enough. As soon as he heard me say that he should catch all the fish, he looked at me, dumbfounded, and asked me what I had meant.

I told him that the oil he had let fall on the ground and the old oil cans and filter would soon be washed into the little pond. The oil would then pollute the pond and begin to kill many of the small fish. Once the small fish were gone, the big fish would die off, and for a time the pond could become sterile. He looked at me in horror, and I could feel his shame and concern. I think that he was surprised that I was not angry, nor did I say these things with any malice. What I had said also surprised me to a point where I was almost speechless.

As quickly as I had appeared at his truck, I said good-bye and disappeared over the ridge. I waited for the better part of an hour but never heard the truck drive off. It had started but once, then quickly stopped, and this made me curious as to what the guy was doing. I suspected that he might be fishing again, taking my advice but missing the greater lesson. He had said that one fish was enough for him, but now I suspected he was going to take more. I slipped back to the edge of the pit, being careful not to make any noise. He would be more cautious now that he knew someone was around the area. I peeked back through the root system and again was shocked by what I saw.

All the oil cans and oil filter had been picked up. The truck was moved back from its original position, and the man was shoveling the contaminated soil into an old five-gallon bucket. I watched him then go to a grove of small pine trees and carefully dig one up, carry it to the hole, and plant it as if he were planting a garden. I realized that my words had moved him and had changed his heart. I was shocked to see how much, for it appeared that the teaching went deep and touched his spirit. The most I could have hoped for would be that he would have just left the area and never dump oil on the ground again. I could not believe that he was so moved that he was actually cleaning it up.

I crept away from the edge and started back to camp as darkness slowly crept over the land. I thought long and hard about the incident at the pit, and suddenly I realized that I had my answer. "Teaching! Teaching!" I screamed. That was the answer to how to live my Vision and to bring that Vision to people. I just had to teach, and teach anytime the opportunity revealed itself. The answer that I had been searching for all this time since my forty-day Vision Quest had finally been answered. It was obvious, too, that the Stalker was following me back to camp, watching me the whole way and trying to distract me from my thoughts.

Once back in camp I was too excited to eat, and I lit a fire to cut through the darkness. It was then that I realized I had not looked at what Grandfather had left for me to see, and he would be back in the morning. I stood from the fire and began to move to his shelter, but as soon as I got to the door I was hit with the most vile stench of death I had yet encountered. I realized then what the symbol on Grandfather's staff was trying to tell me. The Stalker was not concerned with my thoughts or with my practicing my skills. This demon of the mind or imagination did not want me to find what Grandfather had left for me in his shelter. For some reason this demon did not want me to get to the shelter, and it fought me hard.

As I moved closer to the shelter the Stalker stopped using mental or spiritual energy; it was now using physical energy. It was as though I were trying to push through some invisible wall. I struggled and grew angry, but the demon fed on my anger and the wall pushed me back, right to the fire's edge. I then let go of the anger, fell to my knees, and began to pray to the Creator. I prayed out loud, asking that the Stalker be given love, compassion, and healing. As each word was spoken, I could feel the demon leaving, fleeing from the camp area as if running for its very life.

I entered Grandfather's shelter and searched around, finding nothing but a large roll of white buckskin hanging from the lodge pole. I carefully took down the roll and immediately knew that this was what Grandfather had wanted me to see, though I did not yet know what it was. I took it back to the fire so I could get a better look, and I felt the presence of the Stalker, as persistent and strong as ever. I ignored its presence and began to unroll the white buckskin material. To my astonishment it was the robe that I had seen in my forty-day quest and had again seen on Grandfather. I carefully examined the symbols and found that they were the marks of the teaching entities of Earth and creation. I knew that this was the robe of a shaman, an elder, and a teacher.

I stood and began to unfold the robe fully, and the Stalker seemed to fight even harder to steal me away from what I was doing. Without a thought I flung the robe around me, and suddenly he was gone. I sensed a deep peace and broad sense of knowing. I realized again that to live my Vision I had to teach as many people as possible and at every opportunity. But I had to teach without preaching, for preaching would only close off the heart. With this robe, I thought, I could become a good teacher. The robe seemed to hold all the magic, all the wisdom and power of the teacher. But I still could not understand why Grandfather would hold the teacher's robe. Certainly he was a shaman, but his teachings had ended with me and Rick.

Just as I had placed the robe back into Grandfather's shelter and returned to the fire, Grandfather walked into camp. He sat down and smiled at me with a broad grin. Without greeting he began to talk and said, "I hold the robe of the teacher because I teach you and grandson Rick. I also teach whenever anyone will listen. I go to my old friends with the herbs of healing, but I go as teacher even more so. We teach anytime the opportunity becomes manifest in our lives, just as you taught the man with the truck."

"How did you know that I taught him when you were nowhere around?" I asked.

Grandfather answered, saying, "Once you teach someone, you become part of that person and that person becomes part of you. You then have one mind and are fused with the life force. You were there, so I also had to be there.

"We can never walk alone, nor can we be lonely, for we are forever part of the wilderness and part of all our teachers. The world of spirit also teaches us, and thus we become part of that world, fused with the expanded consciousness and 'one' with all things. This demon, the Stalker, is part spirit and part mind. He is the part of you that is afraid to take the robe of the teacher, for that part of you relishes your freedom. To live your Vision is to take away some of that precious freedom and give you the responsibility of teaching others. By giving up part of self and by giving part of self, we become teachers. Thus we heal the Earth and the robe becomes our life.''

''Where did the robe come from?'' I asked.

Grandfather replied, ''The robe is the symbol of a teacher and has no power in and of itself. It is the teacher who gives it power, not the robe that gives power to the teacher. It was owned once by Great-grandfather Thunder, who passed it on to me, and someday I will pass it on to you. But first you must know the power that it symbolizes.''

''But how will I know that I am a teacher?'' I asked.

''You know because that is where your Visions and Vision have led you. You have been chosen by Vision. You have lived what you teach, and you have lived the asceticism of aloneness. All who try to teach without the Vision and without living the skills are false prophets.''

Grandfather quoted an old proverb:

''He who knows and knows he knows is wise: Follow him.
He who knows and knows not he knows is asleep: Awaken him.
He who knows not and knows he knows not is a child: Lead him.
He who knows not and knows not he knows not is a fool: Avoid him.''

I was surprised once again that Grandfather could so freely quote from so many philosophies and religions. I suspected that this saying was from an Arabian proverb, but I have no idea how he came to know it. I understood the importance of having lived skills and asceticism, before attempting to teach them. For a person who tries to teach things he has not lived, is a fool. I understood also that a person should be directed by Vision to teach, for the Vision is the true path of the heart.

"What about the teachers in my school?" I asked. "Did all of them come to be teachers through Vision?"

Grandfather replied, "Some have been led by Vision, others have been led by their hearts, and others have been forced into being teachers. I am sure that you can tell the difference in their teachings. The teaching I speak about is not that of school but of the spiritual things and of skills that have spiritual meaning. You are not teaching simple academic subjects but skills and philosophies that change people's hearts. That is why most religious leaders are led to their places of worship through the visions of the heart."

"You said that someday the robe will be passed along to me," I said. "When will I be worthy of that symbol, or will I ever be?"

"You will be worthy when you practice the physical and spiritual skills that you will one day teach. But practice is not enough, for you must live those skills for many years and they must be your life. You will know in the schools of society, which teachers teach from Vision. You will also know which teachers of wilderness are from Vision and have lived in the wilderness. All others are false prophets, having practiced but never lived the skills. They know not the philosophy of what they teach.

"To know the things of the spirit and the skills of the wilderness, which are sacred, you must live them. You must go to the wilderness, cast all aside, and enter that wilderness naked. You must say to the rocks, 'I know you, help me to make my tools.' You must say to the land, 'Take me, teach me to make shelter, fire, and to feed myself.' Only when a man has given in to wilderness completely and goes there with nothing, and only when he puts his life in Nature's hands for long periods of pure asceticism can he ever know. Once he does this, with Vision, he becomes a teacher. Until that day he can only teach what he has lived to that point.''

Grandfather left camp to pray as soon as the sky grew light, leaving me alone with my thoughts. I understood what Grandfather had told me. Not only did I have to practice my skills but also to live them for long periods of time. I had to live the physical skills, and especially the spiritual skills. It was not enough to go out for weekends and summers into the wilderness. I had to live wilderness for many years, continuously, before I could ever teach. I knew then that someday I would wander and live within the temples of creation, for that was how my Vision would become reality. I could not live my Vision until I had lived the skills and philosophy for a long period of time.

It was comforting in a way to know that I had to go out someday and live all that I had learned. I wanted to wander and to live as I had been taught. What scared me was that someday, too, I would have to pick up the teaching robe and begin to take my Vision to the people. I knew that to stay in the wilderness would not be living my Vision, for I, like everyone else, would someday be responsible for the destruction of the Earth unless the Vision was lived. I touched one person's life that day in the old sand pit, and I hoped to touch others.

10

False Prophets

Grandfather had taught me very early on in life that each person could be a teacher. Not only was Nature our primary source of study and knowledge, but so, too, was all of mankind. He taught us how to look for the teachings in two ways. First, there are teachers who showed us through example and viable working skills. These skills would work all of the time in any conditions and were considered universal. Second, there are teachers who teach us what not to do. By watching their actions you would see that most of the time their skills would not work or would work only in one situation. Though these are opposite in approach, they are both teachers nonetheless and should be respected. In turn, he taught me that whenever you learn from anyone, you also must reciprocate by giving back some of your knowledge; thus the cycle of teaching is complete.

I was forever a student of life, for the whole of creation would teach me, even man. One has to eagerly search out the teachings and many times look beyond superficial meanings, looking deeper to find the truth. I went out of my way to find good teachers. The elderly always fascinated me, so I sought out old people living in the Pine Barrens, even those confined to nursing homes. Our elders are a source of limitless knowledge and inspiration, yet our society throws them away when they can no longer work. The Native American people cherish their elders and put them into an exalted position so they can continue to learn from their extensive knowledge.

I sneaked into many churches, temples, and synagogues, just to learn what was being taught there. I took everything I learned, good or bad, and studied it thoroughly. No matter who was speaking, I listened intently. I would drop my self away and listen purely, not allowing any prejudice to slip in and taint the teaching with thoughts or critical analysis. Later, when the teaching was over, I would bring it back to Nature and decide then whether I could use the new information or not. Many times when I thought something could not possibly work, it worked in the purity of Nature and I had to accept it as true.

In this way, by looking beyond the superficial motions of Nature and man, I could amass deeper knowledge by just knowing how to look. The spirit world became the most profound teacher. No matter if the spirit or demon were good or bad, if I learned from it, then it was good. The lessons and understanding were the most important thing, no matter how you got to that wisdom.

Many times I sought the teaching entities through a process called the Prayer Quest. This quest was undertaken so that the Quester could take a question right to the spirit world and receive an answer on a spiritual level. Unfortunately both good and bad spirits could answer the question, but with some searching you could turn around bad medicine and learn from it.

A Prayer Quest is very similar to a Vision Quest, except for the reason the quest was being taken. Like the Vision Quest, the Prayer Quest was set up in the same way. One was confined to a tight circle without any comforts and with just a small jug of water. The object of the Prayer Quest was to ask for nothing personal but to give thanksgiving for everything. A Prayer Quester could also ask for healings of loved ones but never for himself or herself. About the only thing a Prayer Quester could receive would be some spiritual answers and direction. The Quester stayed in constant prayer day and night, with no time to recuperate. It was believed that by sacrificing this period of time to the spirits and the Creator, the Quester would be deemed worthy and prayers would be answered. Where the Vision Quest gave Visions, the Prayer Quest answered prayers.

I was on the first day of a Prayer Quest and I was praying most diligently for a healing for my brother. Jim had to have some bones fused together in his ankle and now would be in a cast for nearly six months. No one knew if he would even be able to walk correctly again. The injury would certainly keep him out of the woods for a while, and that was bothering him. He loved the woods, and he loved to visit Grandfather, though he was not there every day. This bone fusion could make it so that he could no longer hike the distance from our house to Grandfather's camp. I prayed that day for a healing so that he could once again enter the woods and walk easily.

I prayed well into the night, without ever rising from my knees or lowering my eyes from the sky. I knew that the power of prayer and belief, mixed with love, were the most powerful tools on Earth, and I had no doubt that Jim would walk well again. I finally relaxed and sat back into my quest area to drink some water and to think about some of the things that were still bothering me about my last Vision

Quest. I knew now that the only way to bring my Vision to society was to teach somehow, but I had no power, and people rarely respected some "bum" from the woods.

As I sat in the confines of darkness, thinking about my lack of power, I sensed something coming toward me from the swamp. It was not anything I could identify because sometimes it walked as an animal, then sometimes like a spirit, and a few times sounded like an animal. I was confused and a little frightened. I waited for this thing to draw closer, but it had stopped several yards away from my area and did not move. I could hear its breathing at times, but it did not sound like the normal breathing of either man or beast. Pushing these things out of my mind, I got back to my knees and began to pray for my brother. And the thing began to move again.

I stopped praying and the thing stopped. Now I firmly believed that this was again the Stalker. It seemed that ever since my forty-day Vision Quest, he had been around in one form or another, trying, as always, to remove me from my thoughts. Determined now, I began to pray again, pushing all thoughts of this thing out of my mind, no matter how close it got to me. I refused to let the Stalker break my concentration again. I got lost in my prayer and poured my every thought into it, losing sight of all that was going on around me. I stayed this way for what seemed like hours, until I finally had to take another water break.

As I sat down and opened my eyes, there stood before me a man, or a spirit, I did not know which. He was dressed in semi-modern coat and tie, and about his shoulders was thrown a dark cape. He looked well groomed and very out of place this deep in the woods. It was then that I decided he had to be spirit and not flesh. But he also felt neither good nor bad, more benign in a way rather than anything else. We looked at each other for a long time, and I suppose that I must have looked startled and frightened. He only smiled, and I could feel some form of peculiar power. "Who are you and what do you want?" I asked sheepishly.

He replied, "Do not be afraid." But the feeling of fear and spiritual reservation never left me.

He then said, "I have come to answer your question concerning your Vision."

"But I have no real question," I said.

The spirit then said, "I thought you wanted to know about power and what could empower your Vision."

I was taken back and at a loss for words, mainly because I did not formally ask for power or for answers from the spirit world.

"Did you not think about the power that you would need to reach people and change them?" He asked again.

I said that I did not specifically ask for anything but only for my brother's healing.

"But you were thinking of power," he said. "So I will show you how to get this power, and I can teach you quickly."

The spirit began to speak to me without waiting for my answer. He said, "Real power in the world of society comes from money. Money is all that the people respect, and money is what society worships. Money buys power and people listen to people with money. This society respects people with the power of money, and it is through the power of money that you can reach people. Money will help you gain the power necessary to do what you wish. Money is power, money is respect, and money teaches people to listen."

I answered, saying, "Money is not power, for it is one of the false gods of the flesh. People do not respect money at the level of the heart, thus money becomes useless for things of the spirit. Christ had no riches, nor does Grandfather, so there is no power in money.''

The spirit did not listen but said, ''Then you can get your power to teach and influence through a title. Having a title and a good position in society will make people take notice. It will cause them to listen. The bigger the title and the more powerful the position, the more people will pay attention to what you have to say. Thus your power will come from the position you choose in life.''

Then I replied, ''Like money, the power of position or title has no bearing on the teachings of the heart. These things may reach people of logical mind who live in flesh, but they will never reach the heart and spirit.''

Growing a little perplexed, the spirit continued. ''Then you will find power in the strength of body and in the strength of mind. People will admire a strong body and mind. All great leaders and teachers need strong bodies and minds to impress the masses with their message.''

I said, ''Body and mind are but outward appearances and have nothing to do with the grander things of life. Those who need to listen will not listen to an overeducated mind or an overdeveloped body. What the masses need is sincerity and love, and it makes little difference what kind of package it comes in. It is the spiritual mind and body that need to be strong, and all else will follow. Real strength is in the spirit, and that is what reaches the heart.''

''Fear is also a great power,'' the spirit continued, ''for the power of fear can drive the masses to accept that which you desire.''

I replied, ''Fear may drive the masses, but fear will never drive them to accept. You cannot force anyone into doing or understanding through fear. Fear only becomes a prison to the body but never to the mind and spirit.''

''Then there is power through deception,'' the spirit said. ''You can use the power of deception to lead the masses to the place desired. Then once there, you can keep them in that desired place with more deception.''

"The mind and body can be deceived, but never the heart,'' I replied. "Nothing can deceive the heart or the spiritual mind, so there can be no power in *any* deception, for the heart will know. As I know now that you are trying to deceive me into believing that power is the answer.''

The spirit was now very agitated. "Power changes things. It is the force of change. There is nothing that power cannot reach.''

I answered bluntly. "Only love can change. Only love can create the change that I desire.''

Now in a rage, the spirit turned toward a bush and with the wave of his hand cast it into a blaze of fire, as if to show me his power.

I asked, "Do you need to destroy something beautiful to show your power? What purpose do you have to waste a life in this way? To show me that you have power? If all you can show me is the death of a bush, then I am not impressed by your power. There is no power in senseless and needless death.''

Sensing my animosity toward him, the spirit calmed and said, "There is power in religion. If one rises to the top of religion, then this is power. This religious power can control the masses, and this power can bring you close to God.''

"If religion makes one flourish,'' I said, "then there needs to be no control. If there needs to be no control, then there needs to be no power. Only the Creator can give power, but only power for pure purpose. No church, temple, or religious cult can give anyone this power.''

"There is power in healing,'' the spirit said. "When the masses see the healer, they know that he is powerful, and they will follow. They will listen to what he has to teach.

By gaining power through healing, you also change the masses.''

I said, ''There is no power in healing, for the healer is not the power; he is but a bridge. The power only flows through the healer, and he becomes an empty vessel. This power of healing you speak of is not power at all but the power of show, which boosts one's ego. Ego then diminishes all power.''

Now in a very angry voice the spirit sai., ''You can use power over people and force them to do what you wish. You can force the changes that you want them to have.''

I answered sternly, ''Only the power of love and Vision can help people change. One cannot force someone to change for very long, for forced change brings rebellion. When the change is not forced but comes from each person's heart, there can be no rebellion, for it was their choice.''

The spirit paced back and forth in front of me, growing angry with each step, until finally he shouted, ''You will never see your Vision become reality without this power!''

I replied, ''The power will come from my heart, my love, and my Vision, and I need no other power. Your power is an illusion and at best temporary and weak.''

The spirit looked at me with fury in his eyes and I grew very frightened. From deep within, my spirit spoke and said, ''Go now to your place of power, and I will pray for you, that your lust for power does not consume you.'' With those words the spirit was gone and the landscape returned to the reality of Nature. I began to laugh at the spirit and his stupidity. Certainly I learned from this one, but I learned what not to do. This is the kind of thinking that drives most of society, and I suspect this was its embodiment, found in this spirit of nonsense. I chuckled for a long time. I learned what not to accept, for people who seek that kind of power are eventually consumed by its emptiness.

I kept praying for the next day and night, hoping that the power of love and belief, the real power, would carry my prayers through. The Prayer Quest grew silent, and it felt good to be there. Periodically I thought about the spirit that had entered my area, and the more I thought about it, the more I could see that its power was being used by so many factions in society. In fact, that kind of power ruled the world at this moment. I could now see why there was such destruction to the Earth, why there were wars, hatred, fear, starvation, and a world not worth living in. It was all because of man's selfish lust for this empty power.

I returned to camp, feeling that my prayers had been more than answered. Grandfather sat at the fire, awaiting my return. Without even looking up to acknowledge my presence, he began to speak. "As I have told you, you will encounter many teachers, good teachers and bad teachers. We can learn from both. As you have seen, you have just encountered a bad teacher from the spirit world. This one was a false prophet, for what he taught does not work. You saw through these false teachings and you answered with truth. Thus you learned from the encounter. You learned what not to do. Others would be swayed by his words and mannerisms and accept these teachings without question.

"Many teachings are not so obviously wrong. There is a danger in accepting anything. You should always listen to a teaching purely, and then prove it right or wrong. Nothing should be accepted as law and truth until it is proven in the purity of creation. Some things may take a long time to try and to understand. Some things will not work all of the time or be suitable for each person. What is truth for one may not be truth for another. Each person must then follow his own truth. It is best to seek out simple and universal truths that work for everyone. All else complicates and obscures the real truths in life.

"Beware of the false prophets, for they may distort the truth. You will encounter many as you travel through life. Some false prophets are obvious, yet others are obscure. They come as prophets, religious leaders, teachers, and officials. Beware of their teachings if it conflicts with your heart. Accept nothing that comes from anyone who has not lived what he or she teaches. For there is great danger in listening to those who do not have experience. You cannot know something until you have lived it and tested it out in your heart.

"Some teachings are very complicated and hard to understand. Seek always to simplify, for man likes to complicate simple truths. As I have told you, man takes the simple things of life and tries to complicate them to fit his needs. It is because of this complication that man has turned away from Nature and from spiritual things. As you will see, man's religions and philosophies are the most complicated and confusing. That is why we should always seek the simplicity. Simplify, and life becomes real."

I feel that is one of the quests in Grandfather's life. He seemed to search out the simplicity in the most complicated things. He wandered this country and listened to everything and everyone. Then he would return to Nature and sift for the simple truths. It was by these truths that he lived. I also have become a searcher of simplicity. I believe that much of man's strife comes from needless complications in life, work, and religion. Man pays dearly for this complication and pays with his life. Simplicity is the real treasure in life.

11

The Quest

I was sitting in my Vision Quest circle atop Prophecy Hill. This was my second day of what I wanted to be a ten-day quest. This quest was so important to me because I was in the process of making a decision to go back to South America or up into Alaska. I had been leaning toward Alaska because I had never really been there. In my wanderings I might have come close to the border but had gone no farther. I wanted to build a cabin there and live off the land. Homesteading sounded very enticing, since I had been wandering for nearly ten years and was growing weary of constant travel.

There was also something missing in my life, though I could not identify its source. For the past year my life had been a paradox. At times it would be so empty and at times so full. Certainly I was doing what I wanted to do, and I was living my dream, but I had not yet come to terms with my Vision. I had no idea how I was to live the Vision; in fact, I was beginning to deny it. I felt that I had far too much to learn, and there was no way I could go back to society yet. Anyway, society had nothing that I wanted, nor could I really face its reality anytime I would go back. I had no real skill that could get me a job, I had no education other than high school, and I could not mix with people.

As I sat there I thought back over my life. I had nothing to show for all the years I had spent in the woods, at least not in society's terms. I thought of Grandfather and Rick and how I missed them. I thought of my years as a child and how I avoided most of the things the other kids would find enjoyable. It seemed that my life was a way of avoiding contact with the games of society. I would do only enough to get by, socialize enough so that I would not be considered strange by the other kids. I could tell no one of my life in the woods or of my spiritual quests, for no one would understand. I felt so lonely all those years, for there was no one I could really talk to.

When everyone else was planning college and careers, I was planning the ultimate escape. I couldn't function in the world of society, no matter how hard I tried. All my attempts at returning had met with defeat, and I had a bitterness and contempt for everything in society. I couldn't really understand the workings of man's world, nor the logic behind his games. I had tried and failed to play those games, for they were never right with my heart. To most everyone else I was a bum. Even my folks did not really understand what drove me or even who I was anymore. I was beginning to wonder myself who I was and if I would ever see the reality of my Vision.

I had so much to say, so much to teach, but no one who would really listen. I had spent my entire childhood and ten years of my adult life wandering in wilderness, and now I felt that it was worth nothing. If I could not share what I knew, then so many things would be lost. So many skills that were sacred to Grandfather, to his people, and to me would vanish. I wanted to teach, but I could not face going back to society. Even if there were people who would listen, the act of going back scared the hell out of me. Society and man's towns and cities were as foreign to me as the wilderness was to common man. I could not survive there, for I had none of his skills.

It was my thinking now to decide that I wasn't really ready to go back. I thought that this was the Creator's way of telling me that I still had much to learn. After all, Grandfather had been eighty-three before he began to teach Rick and me, and at twenty-six I still had a long way to go and a lot to learn. I felt that the experience of homesteading in Alaska or the Canadian Rockies would do me good. It would round out my wilderness education and give me a place I could really call my own. I thought that once I had established myself there I could take short trips out into towns and sell some of the crafts I would make. This way I could get a slow baptism back into society without compromising my beliefs.

The theory sounded good in my mind, but there was something that would not agree with my heart. In my travels I had passed through many towns and cities, and I could see the destruction spreading across the Earth like some unchecked cancer. I felt the urgency deep within, but my life was still filled with the denial of my Vision. I felt that I could do nothing, that my voice would never be heard over the crazed rush of society. Anyway, there was no clear path to what I wanted to do to live my Vision. I justified my fear by believing that I had not yet learned enough. I deluded myself into believing that there was still plenty of time. Concerning this point, I denied my Vision, denied the prophecies, and in so doing denied myself.

The second day of this ten-day Vision Quest was becoming very frustrating. It seemed again that Nature and the Creator had turned their backs on me. There were no answers to my questions and no acknowledgment of my prayers. The question of Alaska would not resolve itself, for the more I thought about it, the more my heart would disagree. South America was definitely out of the question. The only thing that seemed to feel good was to go back to my parents' house, though the thought of going back seemed absurd. My mind reeled with all the questions and floundered to find answers, to the point of mental exhaustion.

I had been awake through the first two full days of the quest, and now, as the sky grew dark, I quickly fell asleep. I don't know how long I was asleep, nor was I aware if I had dreamed. I awoke abruptly to the sound of a coyote's howl. With my eyes wide open to the darkness I tried to remember where I was and what I was doing. I had lost touch with reality and now struggled to get it back. I could sense movement in the distance, but it was not of spirit but of animal. I could feel the letdown, for I had hoped something would come to me. The moon had not yet come up, and I strained to see, but the darkness was absolute.

I looked skyward, and to my horror the stars were blood red. It became obvious that this was the reason the night had been exceptionally dark. Fear pounded through my chest, and I could feel my blood pressure rise. All I could think of is that I had to get away. I had to get out of the Pine Barrens and to the farthest outreaches of wilderness to save myself. The Pine Barrens, though thick and largely unknown, were too close to man. I could not believe that it had happened so quickly. I remembered what the prophecy had said, that I had one year to get back to wilderness before the fourth sign became manifest.

As I attempted to stand, all the blood seemed to rush out

of my head, and I staggered back to the ground. An old, familiar voice called to me from the brush, and I looked up to see an old man standing there. He pointed at me and said, ''What have you done, Grandfather, what have you done to me?'' It was the old man from my Vision, coming back again to haunt me.

I answered hoarsely, ''Nothing. I have done nothing to you.''

He replied, ''Nothing. That is what you have done: nothing. Nothing means you have given in to your fear and have become complacent. This, then, is your legacy and your destruction. You have killed your grandchildren because of your complacency, denial, and fear.''

''Noooo!'' I shouted, but my voice just echoed across the emptiness.

The old one, possibly my grandson or great-grandson, had vanished, but the stars still shone bloodred. I realized that it was now too late to do anything. The third sign had come and I had given in to years of fear. I felt so sick, for I had denied my Vision, and now I was here on Prophecy Hill, still trying to put it off, again giving in to my fear. I had been given a chance so many times, and each time I had taken the easy way out. If only I had not given in to the fear, I possibly could have postponed this for even a day. At least I could have tried, no matter how meager I thought that attempt might have been. Now I was as responsible for this destruction as everyone else, for I had done nothing.

I began to cry, burying my head in the dying Earth. I began to sob, for now all was lost, and now the only decision I had to make would be how fast I could get away from inevitable destruction. I lifted my head to the sound of footfalls, and as I lay looking toward the distant horizon I could see a coyote emerging into a clearing. He paused for a moment, then another shadow joined him. Clearly it was his mate. Following her were three little coyotes, obviously a family. They played and frolicked in the clearing, oblivious to the fire in the sky. They seemed so happy and full of life. In their world all seemed complete.

The longing I had felt hit me again, and I found myself admiring this family. I felt that emptiness, and in a strange sort of way I wished that I had a family. It would feel so nice to have someone to talk to who would understand me. The warm touch of a woman I loved would make my life nearly complete. Children to teach and play with would be ecstasy. I lost myself in that thought and felt warm and complete. All the emptiness and longing seemed to disappear for a moment, and my life was full.

As suddenly as the image of a family had come, it was gone. All that was left were the blood-red stars. Even the clouds and the rising moon were red. The horrible realization of never being able to have a family rushed over me. It was something I would never see, now that the night of the bleeding stars was upon me. Even if I met someone, I could not raise a child in a world that was to be doomed. Even if I did escape the ultimate destruction by going deep into the wilderness, those first years would be so hard for a family. I couldn't dream of training anyone for that journey within the year.

I lost myself in my thoughts for a while, paying no attention to the land around me. I was so filled with guilt for not having done something sooner to prevent the third sign. Why had I not been warned and driven out of the woods by the Creator if the end had been so close? Why did it have to come to this before I had a chance to try to do something? I was angry at myself and angry with creation for not warning me sooner. At least I knew now that no child of mine would have to face the destruction of the

Earth and die in the world of cannibalism. The old one who had come to me was not my grandchild, yet he considered me his grandfather.

"We have to pay for the sins of our grandfathers" came a voice, and Grandfather walked into my Vision Quest circle.

"Grandfather," I said, "why was I not warned? Surely you could have come back to me in this way and warned me. Surely the signs of the Earth could have warned me. Now I will never see my Vision live. Now I will have no chance to at least try."

Grandfather smiled and said, "You have been warned." With a wave of his hand across the sky, the stars turned back to their natural liquid silver color and he was gone. "You have been warned, you have been warned" came the voice of Grandfather's spirit again, then all fell silent.

I was in a state of shock and confusion and relieved, for I had a reprieve from the ultimate death sentence. I would have a chance to live my Vision. I fell to the ground and wept like a child. I prayed to the Creator and thanked creation profusely. I had been reborn, and the fires of my Vision Quest had been rekindled. There were no longer any questions, at least no question of where to go. The only question was how I could live my Vision and where I could possibly start. All I knew was that I had to teach someone somehow, no matter how little difference it would make to the overall problems of man.

The images of the coyote family came rushing back to me, along with the feeling of loneliness. Certainly there was a huge difference between being alone and being lonely, and now for the first time in my life I was really lonely. It was a loneliness that simple friendship could not dissolve. I felt a real need for a wife and a family. My life, I knew now, could not be complete as a loner and wanderer. I did not know where this woman would be or how to find her. My life was far different from other lives, and I guessed that very few women would want to share my life. Having a family was as hopeless as finding a way to live my Vision. I did not know where to start.

Then I remembered what Grandfather had once said to me. "Vision, like love, takes no planning, for it just happens. It is directed by the Creator and made manifest by creation. Take no care as to how you will live your Vision or how you will find your love. For the Creator has planned all these things, and the way will become clear to your heart. You have been given a choice, but if you listen to your heart, there needs to be no choice. Your path is your heart, and all that you need do is follow it."

I remained for the last eight days of the Vision Quest, then headed back home to my folks. From there my path would lead me to my Vision and to my love. I have found that the grave mistakes that take place in life are made when a person does not follow his heart. When the heart is ignored, life becomes complicated and distorted, but when the heart is followed, we touch the Creator. Logic and reason are poor alternatives to a life full of love and Vision.

12

Abigail

It was mid-January and I had just finished up a ten-day winter survival and tracking class when the call came in. Lisa, our school secretary, took the call and conveyed the message. I always hated using the telephone, for the telephone was always so distant and impersonal. I liked to face a person when they spoke to me. I had been wandering about the farm, relaxing from the class, and at the same time tracking along the river. I was caught up in some little adventure when she handed me the message. Another child missing, I thought. That would make the sixth child in the last two months and nearly twenty tracking calls I had received in one form or another. I was extremely exhausted from teaching the class, almost wandering around in a daze. There was no way I could take this tracking case. I would have to call in some of my students to do the tracking for me.

Twenty years ago, I thought, I would have considered the child lost in the woods. Now a missing child could mean abduction, and more than half the time, that would be the case. I looked back at the tracks that edged along the river for one last time and headed back up to the house. My mind rushed over all the tracking cases I had had in the past year. The last five children I had found were either lost in the woods or had been abducted. All were found dead. There was a certain bitterness that rose in my throat. I just could not handle finding another child dead. I had seen too much death in my life, tracked too many trails that ended in hopelessness and death. I could also sense the result of a tracking case before I got to the trail, and about this one I sensed death. Even before I reached the house I could feel the hopelessness, and in my state of fatigue I could barely handle the thought. There was no way I could go, I thought.

The woods kill a child or an adult not out of malice or viciousness but without consciousness. Simply, Nature obeys the laws of creation, and anyone alien to the world of the wilderness must die. An abduction, however, is of a world filled with the worst demons of man's mind. It is a world of hatred, evil, obsession, and death. No child is safe anymore, not even teenagers. With the scant information I had about this case it could either be an abduction or a little girl lost in the woods. The information said very little else. As I walked, I dreaded the phone calls I had to make. Talking with parents of a missing child, or loved ones of a missing hiker, is always painful, and I tended to take on their pain. A tracker has to remain objective, aloof, and detached. My heart had never permitted me to be detached, and already the thoughts of the missing girl were starting to hit me deeply.

When I got to the house, Judy's mood was somber. She looked at me with a sense of knowing. She had seen me this way many times before, and she knew what was going on in my mind. The pain of the missing girl became her pain, too, and I could see in her eyes that there was a certain pleading. "Are you going to go look for her?" she asked. I waited for a long moment before answering.

I finally said, "I am going to wait until I talk to the little girl's parents and the police. I've seen too much death. I'm tired from the class, and I don't think that I could help. The girl had gone missing several days earlier, and there have probably been too many searchers. The trail is most likely destroyed." I was very noncommittal and avoided all other questions until I had had time to talk to the parents.

I avoided making phone calls for the next hour, trying to wash away all the negativity in my mind. The procrastination became only a temporary escape, and I could take no more. I told Judy I was going to call some of my students who lived in the area and that most likely they would find the missing girl. After all, my students had excellent records in finding missing children, and I did not hesitate to send them out on calls. This one seemed no different.

Judy looked at me knowingly and said, "You have to go down there and track. I have a feeling about this one, and this feels different. Anyway, you want to go down there. I can see it in your eyes, even though you won't admit it to yourself."

"But—" I began, and she cut me off.

"Go make the phone call," she insisted.

I called the little girl's father. Originally I had been called by the girl's teacher, who had read my books and knew one of my former students. The teacher had called the father and then called me. The phone rang once, and a somber and distraught voice said hello. As soon as I introduced myself, his mood perked up, as if for some strange reason I had given him hope without saying a word. He sounded frantic and drained. As is usual with a parent of a missing child, he'd had no sleep for days and was perched somewhere between hopelessness and confusion. His conversation had to be followed closely, because he would jump from subject to subject. Immediately I could tell that this was a man who loved his child, which was important. I had been on too many tracking cases where the parent had killed his own child and had tried to cover it up with a story about the child being missing. This certainly was not the case here.

The father told me that the little girl had been missing since Tuesday. Today was Friday. He said that his little girl had come back from school and had been playing in their backyard. His wife had gone out to check on her late in the afternoon, and that had been the last time anyone had seen her. He told me that his girl was only six years old, was in the first grade, in a class for the gifted. He said that behind the house were woods and a creek, but he did not think that she would go down there. The little girl had never gone out of the yard before, and he did not think that she really liked the woods. However, he told me of a story she had written about the creek behind the house. The story had been submitted on the Monday, and he suspected that she might have visited the creek that weekend.

What made things worse was that there had been hundreds, possibly more than a thousand, searchers through the area, all of whom had found nothing. Even the sheriff's bloodhounds had stopped at the creek after what they thought might have been a hot trail. No one had turned up anything, and they thought that the little girl, Abigail, had been abducted. The father said that an abduction would be unlikely because where he lived in North Carolina, everyone knew each other, and the family lived at the end of a long dirt road. The father, Ralph, thought that the little girl might have fallen down an old bootlegger's hole and could not get out. Ralph begged me to come down and I could no longer say no.

I went back into the den and glanced at Judy. She asked, "When are you leaving?"

I told her that I had decided to drive and that I would be taking our instructors with me. I did not want to go down there alone. The instructors would be of great value, especially since we would have to pick our way through all the searchers' tracks. I said that my truck was big enough that two of us could drive as two of us slept; that way we could be there at about the same time we would have been if we had flown, and I wanted to get on the road as soon as possible. Judy called Abigail's father and asked him and the sheriff's office not to let the news media know that I was coming. Many times the media would pick up the story that I was coming into an area, and if the girl was abducted, it might send the abductor deeper into hiding.

I called the head instructor for my school, Frank Sherwood, and told him to pack and be ready to track in half an hour. Big Frank had been on many tracking cases in the nine years he has been with me, and he knew the routine. He was also one of the best trackers I had. I also called Frank Rochelle, whom we call Li'l Frank, and told him to pack. He had worked at the school since he was fifteen, and now, after four years with the school, he was a good tracker. At the last minute I got hold of Paul Torres, who had taken nearly half my classes and was helping out at the school as an assistant instructor. I felt that we would make a good team, not only for picking through the searchers' tracks but also for driving down to the track area. There was a good chance we would find her alive, and I wanted all the trackers I could get. Usually I had to wade through the sea of searcher tracks by myself, and this time I would have the best help.

All of us were extremely exhausted from the class, but there were no complaints. The truck was finally loaded, and I said good-bye to Judy and Tommy. Judy said, ''I don't know why, but I feel that this case is going to be very important to you, though I don't know if you will find Abigail alive.''

Tommy said, ''Find her, Daddy,'' and he ran into the house in tears. He knew that I had to go, but I had also just gotten back from being ten days away from home, and he felt that he had to give up his time with me again. Judy assured me that he understood, and we pulled out before dark. With any luck we would be in North Carolina by morning, just as it was light enough to track.

I don't remember if the other guys got any sleep, but I could not sleep at all. My mind was just too active and my adrenaline pumped. I was like an old hound dog about to be set out to track, and I was too wired up. Still, when I had a break from driving, I slipped in and out of sleep, in and out of dream and reality. Most of my thoughts were so distorted from fatigue that I could barely plan the tracking teams and how we would work the area.

Even though Big Frank and I had worked through many tracking cases before, Li'l Frank and Paul Torres would be on their first case. I had no doubts about their tracking abilities, just about how they would work as a team. That usually takes a little work and practice, and we would not have time once we got to the area. We would have to work very quickly. The only thing on my side was that the weather had been unseasonably warm for that time of year, and it would give Abigail a better chance for survival. Time was still important, for this was now her fourth night in the woods, if she was in the woods.

Throughout the whole ride my mind began to think of all the children I had found. Especially those I had found dead. Back when I was living in the wilderness more than a decade before, I was not as deeply disturbed as I was now. It wasn't only because I had my own child now but because I could no longer escape to the purity of the woods. There in the wilderness I could purge myself of all the tracking cases and focus on other things. Now I had the school, and lost people had become a big part of my life. I had not grown callous about it but bitter and angry. I could not understand why anyone had to die in the woods. I also could not understand the disease of abduction, which seemed to be sweeping the country like an unchecked cancer. With those bitter thoughts still vivid in my mind, we arrived at the tracking site.

We slipped by the cameras and went straight to Abigail's house. The most important thing at this point was to find more information about Abigail's disappearance and to meet the men from the sheriff's department. As I walked to the house my mind flashed back to the many cases I had had when I was young, in which the police were skeptical about trackers. Certainly there were law-enforcement agencies across the country that still did not believe in trackers, but with my reputation and the reputation of the people I had trained, things were certainly easier. Many times a police department does not like the fact that an outsider can do what they cannot do, and they tend to resist that possibility. Many times I would have to wait until all law-enforcement efforts had been exhausted before they would agree to send me in, and then it was usually far too late.

Fortunately this sheriff's department wanted any help they could get. They were interested in what I could do with tracking, and to my amazement several of the locals and some of the deputies had read my books. The sheriff, Walter Burch, was delighted that I came all the way down and listened intently to what we had to say. He gave me

several of his men to help with the tracking and communications. Two of his men were excellent trackers, and that
added greatly to my search efforts. They also gave me full
rein and kept the media away while we worked. I could not
have asked for a better group of people to work with. Hope
emerged once again.

I was taken into the house to meet Abigail's family and
to get the remainder of the details concerning the missing
girl. Abigail's father looked drawn and exhausted, and her
mother was on the edge of an emotional breakdown. It is
hard to convey the emotion of the family of a lost child.
There is always so much hopelessness, especially after the
child has been missing for several days. I asked the usual
questions about Abigail, trying to develop physical and per-
sonality profiles. That way the tracking would be easier, for
at times a tracker must become, and think like, the person
he is tracking. I also asked for one of Abigail's old shoes
so that I could get the track-pressure releases that would
become Abigail's fingerprints in the soil. They handed me
a little slipper.

I held the slipper in my hand and examined the pattern
of pressure releases and the size. I had held so many little
shoes in my hand over the years, and I remember all of
them. Out of the nearly six hundred tracking cases of one
sort or another that I had been on in my life, I always
remember the little shoes. As I held Abigail's slipper I felt
her frailty, and tears filled my eyes. The little girl was either
lost in the woods or abducted, and this was the last link in
the mystery and the beginning of the trail. Before I asked
the father any more questions, I had to regain my composure and separate myself from that slipper. I could not get
emotionally involved, for it would cloud my objectivity. I
put the slipper in my pocket and headed into the yard.

The sheriff's men, my trackers, and Abigail's father

talked for the better part of an hour. It turned out that the creek that ran behind the house was full of chemical pollution and a sea of garbage. On the other side of the stream, just a mile away, was a huge garbage dump. The bloodhounds had taken the police to that stream the day before and stopped by the path leading along the stream. They had located no other trail, nor had the hundreds of local searchers turned up anything. Her trail seemed to have vanished. It was also obvious, since a dive team had searched the stream twice, that they felt that Abigail may have been abducted.

I had my trackers search the yard and they turned up several good tracks. They matched Abigail's size and track pattern and gave me a good sense of her track. The difficulty began when we tried to work the front of the house and the TV cameras began rolling. I could not take the chance of letting my name or ability be known to the media. If Abigail was abducted, I did not want her abductor to panic.

It was at this time that I saw another person tracking, but it was not one of our party. His mannerisms and walk indicated to me that he had been trained in my school. It was then that I recognized him. Henry Brown had been through my school several years earlier and had been instrumental in getting me to come down and search. My heart jumped, for now I had another tracker to join our group, a tracker who also knew the land very well and a person who could give me a tracker's opinion of the situation, for he thought as we thought. More hope welled up in my heart.

I searched along the creek for more than an hour, trying to read through the hundreds of searchers' tracks that led along the bank. Finally I found her track, and there was no mistake. It was a track from early in the weekend, indicating that she had been at the creek. I remembered the little story about the creek she had written for school. "I know a place called Buffalo Creek," as her story began. Now there was confirmation that she had been there. Up the creek, and still in full view of her house, one of my trackers found another track. That track I dated as Monday. Then finally I found another track, and that track was made on Tuesday afternoon, about the time she had been reported missing. Also near her track was a man's track, made at about the same time.

I realized then that Abigail's father had been wrong about her not loving Nature. The tracks around the house showed that Abigail took an interest in all the little plants and wild places in her yard. Her tracks also showed an exploration of the creek on Saturday, Monday, and finally on Tuesday. She had been down there before many times and appeared to know the creek well. However, the man's track that was found by hers raised some very serious questions in my mind. Generally a tracker accepts nothing unless proven by the tracks, and it is wrong to assume anything. I did have to alter my opinion of the trail, for there had been someone there at the same time she had been. Whether they saw each other or not, that remained a question.

I began searching along the creek for other tracks and found several upstream and several more downstream. I felt at the time that there was no way that a six-year-old girl could cross the stream, for the waters were deep in places, and just a few high and slippery logs afforded any kind of bridge. The creek was not pristine because it ran from the dump. It stank of chemicals that made the eyes burn, and the bottom was not visible even where the water was a few inches deep. The banks and logjams were strewn with debris, with some parts of the stream nearly choked. Tires, aluminum cans, plastic, Styrofoam, washing machines, and other debris were also found. It was more of a sewer than a creek, but it had fascinated Abigail nonetheless. Possibly she could look beyond the garbage and see hidden beauty. The creek gave me a very uneasy feeling.

I began to get a partial trail that had been made on that Tuesday. Most of her tracks had been destroyed by the searchers, but with the tracking teams we picked our way through the rough spots. It wasn't the most difficult trail I had followed, nor did I get upset, for it was normal to come to a case where the tracks of a missing person were destroyed by searchers. I could not expect anyone but a tracker to be track-conscious. Her tracks led in a huge circle from the river, through some deep woods, and back to her yard, and then disappeared again.

There now seemed to be three possibilities: abduction; being trapped but alive in an old moonshiner's hole; or she was in the creek. I began to search around the upper stream area, since the lower portion had led me in a circle. I found two of her tracks upstream and behind a house, but no more. These tracks had also been from the weekend. Near the tracks was a pile of freshly turned dirt, and a strange feeling came over all of us. Fresh dirt could be a grave, and we wanted no stone unturned. Digging into the dirt, we found several dogs and other animals, burned and decapitated. One of the sheriff's men turned to me and said matter-of-factly, "Looks like Satan worshipers may have buried these."

I shuddered to think that Abigail had been in this area that weekend. Now another possibility entered my thoughts. There was, here in the pile of charred animals, the possibility that she had been abducted. I thought this could potentially explain the man's footprint found near hers on that Tuesday afternoon. We intensified the search of the area but found no other clues. We abandoned the area but not the thoughts and followed the creek back to Abigail's house. We wanted to have a meeting with the sheriff and the other staff to lay out what we had found and to plan our next search. The whole search team was at the meeting, Sheriff Burch, Major Linthicun, Sergeant Forrest, and Deputies Jim Zimmerman and Jim Church, as well as my trackers.

I told them what I was feeling about the tracks. Abigail had known the creek well because she had been there several times, and her tracks showed that she knew where she was going. I told them about the circle I had run, the pile of burned dog carcasses, and that there were no searchers who had found any evidence. I thought that she could be trapped in a pit, abducted, or in the creek. The area had been searched far too well, even the creek, so she must be hidden somewhere. All tracks that I had found were tracks of play and had shown no fear or fatigue. However, most of the tracks had been destroyed by searchers.

As we sat talking, a searcher brought in Abigail's hat. But the hat had been found on the other side of the stream. Hardly anyone had searched there, for none of the searchers, not even myself, could believe that Abigail could have gotten across that creek. We ran to the area where the hat had been found, and finally I found a trail, a trail from late Tuesday afternoon. There had been only a few searchers, and I had my first string of clear tracks, which showed that Abigail was still playfully exploring the creek banks. I asked to have all searchers removed from the woods so that the good trail would not be destroyed. The trackers and I desperately followed her trail to an old building, trying to beat the oncoming dark. The last track I found was in the building; those beyond had been destroyed by searchers the previous day.

We decided to break track and get back to camp. There

was no way I would go on at night. In so many other cases we would keep following the track throughout the night, but the complication of searchers' tracks would make it almost impossible to follow this track in the dark. As we traveled back along the creek, full dark enveloped us. It was an eerie walk, for distances appeared distorted, the baying of feral dogs at the dump echoed through the mind, and I could sense the terror that little girl had felt when she became lost. The final tracks I found showed signs of fatigue, and worse yet, Abigail knew that she was lost. These same sounds must have filled her head that night.

It had been hard to tear myself from the trail, for there was a chance that she was still alive out there somewhere. If she was alive she would have to spend another cold night in the woods, but I could do nothing. I needed sleep; the survival class and two days without sleep were beginning to take their toll on my mind and body. I would rather return to the track fresh and strong, for now we had a good trail I could follow all the way.

However, there would be no sleep for me that night, for my mind was filled with images of Abigail freezing to death in the woods. If we found her the next day and she had died that night, then I would be responsible. It would have been the frailty of my body and mind that would have killed her. I'd had to live with that so many times before, for even body control runs lean beyond exhaustion. At least the night was not that cold. If she was still alive she had a chance. *If she was still alive* became the gnawing question, and I began to have doubts. My mind always finished at the creek, as if being drawn there by some unseen spiritual force.

The next day we rushed out into the field and back to the building. As soon as it was light enough we began to pick our way through the sea of searchers' tracks, finding bits and pieces of Abigail's track, which told us that she was heading for the dump. Big Frank called out to me that he had found a clear track, right at the base of the dump. We ran, and even before seeing the track up close I knew it was Abigail's. The track had been made late Tuesday night, at that time the moon would have been up, and her tracks were heading straight for the top of the dump pile. Now there was obvious fear and confusion in her tracks. She was at this point hopelessly lost, exhausted, and out of her mind with fear.

It had been difficult for the sheriff's men to keep the cameras back and people out of the area. They did a good job, and only a few people came wandering through. As we followed her trail up the mountain of buried garbage, I could see the panic in Abigail increasing, and atop the hill, the first signs of shock. Her tracks showed that she fell frequently, wandered in tight circles, and jumped over things that were not really there. Then the tracks were leading back to the river. My stomach grew sick, for now there was no doubt that she had slipped into the creek. Li'l Frank, Paul, Jim Church, and Jim Zimmerman ran that trail like professionals. I just needed to confirm them. So much better than tracking alone, I thought.

In Abigail's mind that night she must have found some little glimmer of hope, for her tracks straightened and headed directly to a rock pile. There was strong evidence that she sat on the rock pile for a while looking at the creek in the moonlight. Beneath the rocks was a thick tangle of logs and huge rafts of floating garbage. Jim had told me that the divers had not come down this far in their search of the creek. I went down the steep bank to the logjam, and at the last point of the land I found the final track. Abigail had come this way. I lay a little slipper by the track and had a match. Tears flowed from my eyes; I knew the rest.

I walked out onto the log and found some scrapes, dirt, and a partial muddy print from Abigail. Then all was wiped clean from a rush of water. I gazed into the thick sea of garbage, in some places it was nearly four feet thick. I stood for a long time on the log, fighting tears, then I cast a glance back up to Big Frank. He just shook his head in agreement, for no words needed to be spoken. I had found the last track and would now have to leave the rest to the divers. They would find her, but I would suggest how.

We went out the back end of the dump, stepping over garbage, dead dogs and cats, and through the thick woods that bordered the dump. Finally back to Abigail's house where we sat down for a meeting. Hundreds and hundreds of searchers had been awaiting our return and wanted to go and search. I avoided Ralph's questions, and headed straight to the camper that was search headquarters. The media knew who I was now and had pressing questions. The people had been nice, and helpful, but the news I carried with me into that meeting could only be given to the sheriff and those in charge. I told the sheriff that Abigail was in the creek and probably her body was in the log- and garbagejam. I felt that she had looked across that mass of logs and garbage late Tuesday night and thought that it would be an easy way to get across. She was wrong. The sheriff said that his divers had searched that area, but I told him that they did not go down far enough. He asked me what I thought had killed her, and there was a long period of silence. I told him that it wasn't panic, yet she was in a panic. I told him that she could swim and the water would not have been cold enough to hold a swimmer, even a swimmer only six years old. I told him that the garbage had killed her, by entangling her and preventing her escape. In essence, I said, society killed Abigail, because they threw the garbage into the creek. It was not Nature that killed Abigail, but man's garbage.

I told the sheriff that it might be a good idea to send out all the searchers to comb the landscape, just in case we might find some clue as to why she got lost. Certainly they would not find Abigail, for she was hidden in the water and garbage. We went out of the camper, and the sheriff and I told the people what we had found. Then we sent the mass of searchers into the woods, and the sheriff contacted the dive team. All the searchers were kept away from the place of death. I faced the cameras and newspapers for a short period of time and then began to prepare to go home.

Jim Zimmerman and Jim Church seemed a little disappointed at our decision, and asked us to stay. I told them that our work was done, and that we could do no more. I could not handle seeing another child's body being pulled from a watery grave. I had seen too much of that in my life. I said good-bye to Ralph and Vicki Blythe, Abigail's parents, but I did not want to answer their questions. I suspect that they knew for Ralph said, "We need to know, one way or the other. It will be painful, but anything is better than never knowing." I hugged them both and told them I would pray for them. They would know soon enough.

I said good-bye to the sheriff and his people. All of them had made my job much easier. They were one of the most professional but compassionate groups of people I had ever worked with. I told the sheriff that I wanted some of his men to come to my school for several classes, and he agreed. I also thanked all of the searchers I could find. They, too, had been professional and compassionate, taking time out of their lives to really help someone. I could feel the love this community had for each other. Like so many other communities, they had given of themselves.

We quickly got into the truck and left North Carolina. Not a word was spoken, for there was no need for words. We all knew what the dive team would find when they searched that pile of watery garbage. Again I could not sleep and decided to drive most of the way home. I wanted to pass all thoughts of the track and Abigail out of my mind, for I could not handle another child's death. If only she had survived, I thought. If only I had been called in there on Tuesday, when she was first missing, I know that I could have found her. With no searchers' tracks, I know I could have run over her trail. If, If, If . . . but that was not the reality.

As the night grew late and the miles passed, my mind began to think of her death. She could have lived if she had only had a little survival training. Training would have given her the savvy and the shelter to last until the next morning. If only that garbage had not been at the logjam, there could have been a chance that she could have pulled herself out. The garbage killed her. The garbage of society and man's wasteful and complacent attitude. What bothered me was that for the first time in my life I bore witness to the pollution of society directly killing a little child. Society had killed her, there is no doubt.

I began to think about my school and the hopelessness of my quest to change people's attitudes toward the wilderness. The more I looked around me, as I drove, the more garbage, pollution, and madness I saw. My school, my books, and my teachings seemed to be making no difference. The more I thought about it, the less I saw my school as doing any good. I vowed that when I got home I would make plans to shut down the school and move my family to the Canadian Rockies, away from all the madness. At least there, my little boy would not have to face a sea of garbage. The thought of shutting down the school, and the garbage that killed Abigail lay heavy on my heart. I felt a depression sweep over me. We are a society that kills its grandchildren to feed its children, and now we are killing our children.

I had tried to stop the madness through my school, but now it felt hopeless. There was no way that my small voice could reach the masses and teach them that there was a better way. Then I thought about all the other children killed by pollution and society, though not in such obvious ways. How many children, I thought, die each year of cancers that come directly from toxic chemicals, or how many children had been abducted by criminals who are products of the madness of society. These are the silent killers. The problems seemed so immense, so impossible, and there seemed to be no solutions. People had to change before society could change, and I didn't see my school reaching people.

It was early in the morning when I finally dropped off all the instructors and arrived home. I told Judy the story, but I did not tell her that I was thinking about shutting down the school. By my mood, she could tell that the case had hit me very deeply, deeper than all the others. She said, "I told you that this case would be different. Look at you, it's eating your soul. None of the cases you have had so far this year have shaken you so badly." I moped for a few hours, putting off the phone call to Ralph until I could compose myself.

Finally, I gave the family a call and Ralph answered the phone. I told him who I was and he broke down in tears, saying, "Thank you, thank you." He continued, voice broken and trembling, saying "They pulled her out of the creek just a few moments after you left last night. They found her exactly where you said they would."

I could take no more. I broke down and sobbed along

with him. All of my anger and pain seemed to come out during that moment, yet I tried to comfort him as best I could. However, I knew that there could be no comfort. He said, ''Please do not stop what you are doing. It has been a blessing to us all that you went out of your way to help. There are few people like you left in this world, and we thank you.''

He went on to say how Abigail's death had been in vain, that she had died senselessly, without purpose. I told Ralph that Abigail's death would never be in vain, for I would tell her story someday in one of my books and if her story saved another child's life then her death had power. I told him that I would use Abigail's story in my classes, as a teacher. The father sincerely thanked me and said, ''I only wish that your knowledge had gotten here a while ago. Then there might not have been so much garbage in the river. I hear that people are going to start cleaning it up, but it took the death of my little girl to make them change their minds.''

I got out of the house and went for a walk. My mind was beyond fatigue, and my emotions went out to Abigail's family. I was tormented by the fact that I desperately wanted to close my school. I was frightened because I then would not be living my Vision. But what good was my Vision doing for anyone. It certainly didn't help Abigail. If it had then she would be alive today. I felt depression sweep over me as I struggled for answers. This thing did not even make sense in the spirit world, and a deep sense of loss filled me. I, too, had lost Abigail, almost as if she were my own child.

I began to walk out of the woods and at the edge of the yard, Judy met me. She looked at me knowingly and said, ''Now you are thinking of closing down the school, because you feel that you're not reaching people. Well, how about all the letters that come in to the school? You have touched their lives. What do you think your students do when they go back to society? Don't they become warriors for the Earth, and aren't they making a difference? The trouble is that you do not see the outcome of all this. The power is now part of the spirit-that-moves-in-all-things, and soon many more changes will occur. It just takes time. You can't run away from your Vision; your heart won't let you. Where could you run to? If you just reach one person, after these eleven years of classes, isn't that enough?''

I had no answer; there was no need to answer. Judy was right and I had been wrong. She continued, ''Abigail's death should teach you and add energy to your Vision. It should not beat you. Abigail has taught you so much, but you are so close to feeling sorry for yourself that you can't see the lessons. The lessons should teach you to work harder to fight the problems that killed Abigail, other children, and possibly someday your children. A true warrior doesn't run, but learns from a setback, and charges on. That's the kind of warrior I married.''

All my classes now know the story of Abigail. Even this book is written in her memory. Though I don't talk about it much, Abigail still teaches me and adds fire to my lectures. She has driven me to try to reach more people, and to teach more children. Wherever I go, she is on my mind, for her death is a physical manifestation of all the things I fight to change. She, a little six-year-old girl, will always remain one of my greatest teachers. I told Ralph the truth; her death will not be in vain.

13

Wilderness Mind

Living within the strangling confines of society, so that one's Vision becomes reality, is the real quest in a Vision. This is the most difficult time in a person's life, and a nearly impossible path to follow. It is a lonely path, for there are no temples or congregations to lend support. Few speak the language of wilderness and those of the wilderness mind find themselves alone in a land that does not speak their language or understand them. It would be all too easy to run back to the wilderness, for there is peace and reality. It would also be easy to become part of the society we must live within, for to give in is to have no conflict. To live one's Vision one cannot run back to wilderness, nor can we condone the society we hope to change. We must be fence walkers, living between two worlds. This then becomes the razor's edge.

But there is a way to live within the confines of society, thus live the Vision of a better world, without being trapped or isolated. I call this way of living, "the wilderness mind." It makes little difference whether a person has to live in a city, town, or country setting, or whether a person has to work in a factory, hospital, or construction site. The mind is the ultimate freedom, and we are not imprisoned by the place we live or where we work. We have choices in life, especially choices as to the way we think and how we view the world. It is these choices and these thoughts that make life ecstatic or debilitating.

For those of us who have a Vision to see this world change, we have no choice but to work within society to bring about this change. We are tired of the pollution, the wars, the hatred, the prejudice, and the constant destruction of the Earth. We can see beyond the trappings of the flesh and into a world of spiritual riches. There is more for us in life than the nine to five work ethic and a life of clocks, finances, and shallow living. We are governed by a strong Vision to get people back to the Earth, to basic and real values, and closer to the world of spirit. Those with Vision know that they cannot run away and hide, for there is no place to hide. We know that we must bring our Vision back to society or we become responsible for the destruction of the Earth.

Each of us works to change things in our own capacity and own way. I tell my students that they are the ones who carry the Vision, Grandfather's Vision, from my school. They are the ones on the front lines and must face the masses, the complacency and ignorance of society. If they leave my school and do nothing, then the Vision dies, but if they reach just one person the Vision lives. Each person has the ability to lead another back to the Earth and to the Creator. One does not have to abandon job, house, and family to do this as the disciples had to do to follow Christ. Each person has an opportunity every day to reach and teach someone. With each person who returns to the Earth, the Vision of a better world grows stronger, and the spirit-that-moves-through-all-things becomes changed.

There is no doubt that we are in the final days of the Earth as we know it. We have sacrificed our own mother for the sake of the false gods of the flesh. We all work for only four things in life: lasting peace, boundless joy, limitless love, and a purpose beyond ourselves. Society teaches that we have to find these things outside of ourselves, while in fact these things can only be found within. It is the greed of society and its relentless pursuit of the false gods of the flesh that has destroyed and will continue to destroy the Earth. Truly we are a society that kills our grandchildren to feed our children, and I do not foresee much change in that attitude.

Many of us, from all walks of life, philosophies, cultures, and backgrounds, see that we are losing the Earth. Even though we all may not agree with each other, we are still fighting the biggest battle in history. If we do not win the battle, then all is lost and Grandfather's prophecies become reality. There can be no running away and no rest for those fighting the battle. It was once said, "On the plains of hesitation lay the blackened bones of countless millions, who at the dawn of victory lay down to rest, and resting, died." There can be no rest for those of us who love the Earth, our children, and our grandchildren. There is no running away for those who really love, for love is the greatest power. We are part of the life force of this world, and when one part is sick, all is sick.

Fortunately, I can see and feel the resurgence of the spirit mind and people moving closer to the Earth. It is not just a fad, but an undercurrent in today's society. People are growing concerned. New laws are being passed, there are demonstrations and various groups trying to protect the Earth. But this is not enough for we must begin to reach everyone and reach them quickly. We must reach people, not in the mind, but in the heart. For society to change, each person must change. Society must learn to sacrifice its gluttonous lifestyle, greed, and prejudice, to seek the riches beyond the flesh. However, until that battle is won many of us must leave the wilderness and live our Vision. Living in society does not have to consume us, nor drive us from our path.

First, we must realize that the biggest demon we face in society is that of distraction. Society tries desperately, but unconsciously, to take us from our path and from our spiritual mind with its many distractions. We must never give power to these distractions, but always keep our hearts working for our Visions. Many distractions slip into our lives unnoticed, and many come thundering in. Some even try to destroy our faith and purpose. The key here is, as always, awareness. We cannot afford the luxury of letting down our guard, for to do so even for a moment, will cause us to fall and perhaps never get up. We must identify these distractions and then ignore them, fight them, or drive them away.

I have seen many good people, including myself, distracted from the Vision either temporarily or forever. So many have fallen into the trap of chasing the false gods and have begun to play society's game. I have learned through trial and error not to play the game but to ignore it, for it has no relevance to a life of Vision. To play the game of society is to compromise one's beliefs, and to distort the reality of spiritual life. I have found that the best way to transcend the trappings of the game is to stand back and view it from afar, never becoming involved, for involvement is to sacrifice part of the self. Many will not like the fact that you do not play the game, and you will find yourself in a world of mindless critics. Remember, critics are people who usually do nothing. The people who are being criticized are the doers and have no time to be critical of others.

Games and criticism also come from those who think they are working to heal the Earth, but have no real Vision. These pseudo visionaries and false prophets do very little other than criticize and teach skills they have never lived. These people should be avoided but never criticized, for even if the work they do is of little power they are at least working for a better world. These people should be humored at best, or better yet ignored, for the distraction of their bitching and complaining can become a demon.

Beware also of the false prophets and teachers. They may promise you skill and spiritual abilities, but they rarely deliver. There are many of these kinds of people waiting to take in those of society who are lost and searching. They make grand promises, but the followers never come away with any usable skill or insight. Many of these people are self-proclaimed healers and teachers, but they never lived a life of asceticism or gave their lives to their skills in the purity of the wilderness. As Grandfather said, "Those false prophets can be identified by their lack of awareness, for awareness is the doorway to the things of the spirit." Your Vision is unique to you and you need no quick method of enlightenment, for there are no quick ways.

Society can also teach us to grow complacent. We will eventually ignore the destruction and other things wrong with this society. We will rush through life at society's maddening pace and no longer observe. Our complacency will breed inactivity, which will lead to paralysis of body, mind, and spirit. Not seeing a problem or ignoring it will not make it go away or make it better. It will only make the problem worse, for to give the demon of complacency power is to empower the problem. Complacent people do not make good warriors, for they have lost their Vision, or their Vision has been obscured by complacency.

The reality here is that we must live our Vision and share it with other people. This is the way our Vision finally lives. To hide in wilderness is to also hide from the self, and from the Vision. The real quest begins when we come out of wilderness to teach. It is not only a quest to educate, but to stay on the path of Vision when all around is chaos, spiritual death, and distractions. But this does not have to be pain or suffering, for our numbers are growing stronger. Lines of separation are being broken down and there are more people to talk to. As always, we have the power of the wilderness mind.

For those of us who are living our Visions every day, we must create an island in our mind. This is the seat of the wilderness mind which keeps us from being sucked into society's madness. Even though we must live in a world near society, we can create that island of thought in which our conscious and spiritual mind are always thinking of the wilderness, the purity, and the spirit. In the times of need we can go back to the spiritual mind, which is directly connected to all of creation. Thus, with a shift in thinking, we become wilderness again even in the heart of a big city. We are at once part of creation and creation is part of us. There is no inner or outer dimensions and no separation of self, only a perfect oneness. The island of the mind then becomes fused with wilderness.

In times of need we must also seek out wilderness, no matter in what form it comes to us. It could be a prolonged trip into a grand wilderness area that replenishes our spirit and heals our soul, or it could be just a blade of grass growing between the cracks in the sidewalk of some huge city; both are doorways back to the Earth and to purity. Nature is all around us, whether in the city or in the suburbs, all we must learn to do is to use the doorway it provides and find our way back. All prophets, visionaries, and teachers must get back to the purity of wilderness periodically. It must be scheduled, as everything else is scheduled, into our lives. We must stick to our schedule, for that is where we find renewal, answers to our questions, and directions for our Visions.

Above all, we must learn to live our Vision, so there is nothing else in our lives but that Vision. Our families and friends must become part of our Vision, with their personal Visions blending with ours, creating a more powerful Vision. That Vision must be lived beyond self, and we must work from the place of love. To work for self alone is a shallow and hollow form of existence. To reach out and help others, even when it exhausts us, is to live the Vision of love. To work beyond the self is to find one of the true meanings of life, the meaning of love.

This path is not easy. Everyone falls now and then, but we shake ourselves off, learn from our mistakes, laugh a little, and then get right back up. Certainly all of us work hard for the Vision of a better Earth and a life close to the riches of spirit. We work to stop the wars, to stop the polluting, to stop the killing, and to stop the destruction of the Earth as we know it now. Things will get better if we all work hard and if we all love hard and laugh hard. This was not just Grandfather's Vision, nor is it just my Vision, but it is the Vision and the quest of anyone who wants to heal the Earth and love all of creation, including man.

14

Journey From Wilderness

The journey has been long and difficult. The most impossible journey I have made in my life. It is truly the most difficult task that a man or woman must face, for it is the real quest to any Vision. It becomes so easy to compromise beliefs and to stray off the path of the Vision. It is all too easy to get caught up in the rush of society, and to deny the heart. So many times I have fallen, and so many times I have been beaten by my own mind and by society. The laws of society are so different than the laws of creation, for truly they are two separate realities.

I have found that people think with their heads, their wallets, and their egos. I find that the gods that society worships are sex, power, and money, and there is little room for anything else. Society is a demon which removes the individual from what life is all about. Society feeds on people, and people feed society with their lives, their happiness, and their spirits. Society is also a prison, shackling people to live lives of desperation just to get by. Society judges happiness in how much one can accumulate, and people waste their lives in that accumulation. They seem never to have a chance to enjoy life for they must constantly work to preserve all that they have accumulated.

I find that anyone can live in society and blend into the general population. The difficulty comes when someone tries to live a Vision that is foreign to the thinking of society. There are people who do not believe in wars or hatred. There are people who do not believe that life is just nine to five, and that there is more to life than just the accumulation of goods. There are people who believe that the Earth should be healed, and that there is more to life than flesh. There are people who believe that life here could be far better, richer, and fuller, that life can and should be lived close to the Creator and to creation.

There are many people who believe that the real meaning in life is to make a better place for their children and grandchildren. A place where the water runs pure, the forests grow strong, and where life is full of boundless love, lasting peace, limitless joy, and a grand purpose. Many people will not live their Visions because of fear, thus they deny their Vision. If society is to ever change, then each person must live his or her Vision. It is then that the spirit-that-moves-through-all-things will turn the tide of man's destruction. We all must make that journey, if not for ourselves, then for our grandchildren.